Christmas with
Grandma Elsie

The Original Elsie Classics

Elsie Dinsmore
Elsie's Holidays at Roselands
Elsie's Girlhood
Elsie's Womanhood
Elsie's Motherhood
Elsie's Children
Elsie's Widowhood
Grandmother Elsie
Elsie's New Relations
Elsie at Nantucket
The Two Elsies
Elsie's Kith and Kin
Elsie's Friends at Woodburn
Christmas with Grandma Elsie
Elsie and the Raymonds
Elsie Yachting with the Raymonds
Elsie's Vacation
Elsie at Viamede
Elsie at Ion
Elsie at the World's Fair
Elsie's Journey on Inland Waters
Elsie at Home
Elsie on the Hudson
Elsie in the South
Elsie's Young Folks
Elsie's Winter Trip
Elsie and Her Loved Ones
Elsie and Her Namesakes

Christmas with Grandma Elsie

Book Fourteen of
The Original Elsie Classics

Martha Finley

CUMBERLAND HOUSE
NASHVILLE, TENNESSEE

Christmas with Grandma Elsie
by Martha Finley

Any unique characteristics of this edition:
Copyright © 2000 by Cumberland House Publishing, Inc.

Published by Cumberland House Publishing, Inc.,
431 Harding Industrial Drive, Nashville, Tennessee 37211.

Cover design by Bruce Gore, Gore Studios, Inc.
Photography by Dean Dixon Photography
Hair and Makeup by Calene Rader
Text design by Heather Armstrong

Printed in the United States of America
1 2 3 4 5 6 7 8 – 04 03 02 01 00

CHAPTER FIRST

IT WAS ABOUT THE middle of November. There had been a long rainstorm, ending in sleet and snow, but now the sun was shining brightly on a landscape sheeted with ice. The walks and roads were slippery with it, every tree and shrub was encased in it, glittering and sparkling as if loaded with diamonds, as their branches swayed and tossed in the wind. At Ion, Mrs. Elsie Travilla stood at the window of her dressing room gazing with delighted eyes upon the lovely scene.

"How beautiful!" she said softly to herself. "And my Father made it all. 'He gives snow like wool: He scattereth the hoar frost like ashes. He casteth forth His ice like morsels.'

"Ah, good morning, my dears," as the door opened and Rosie and Walter came in together.

"Good morning, dearest mamma," they returned, hastening to give and receive the affectionate kiss with which they were accustomed to be greeted at the beginning of a new day.

"I'm so glad the long storm is over at last," said Rosie. "It is really delightful to see the sunshine once more."

"And the beautiful work of the Frost King reflecting his rays," added her mother, calling their attention to the new beauties of the ever-attractive landscape spread out before them.

Both exclaimed in delight, "How beautiful, mamma!" Rosie added, "It must be that the roads are in fine condition for sleighing. I hope we can go today, mamma."

"Oh, mamma, can't we?" cried Walter. "Won't you give us a holiday?"

"I shall take the question into consideration," she answered with an indulgent smile. "We will perhaps discuss it at the breakfast table, but now we will have our reading together."

At that very time, in her boudoir at Woodburn, Violet and Captain Raymond were also discussing the state of the roads and the advisability of dispensing with school duties for the day that the entire family might enjoy the rather rare treat of a sleigh ride.

"You would enjoy it, my love?" he inquired.

"Very much—in company with my husband and the children," she returned. "Yet I would not wish to influence you to decide against your convictions in regard to what is right and wise."

"We will go," he said, smiling fondly upon her. "I cannot bear to have you miss the pleasure—nor the children either, for that matter—though I am a little afraid I might justly be deemed weakly indulgent in according them a holiday again so soon. It is against my principles to allow lessons to be set aside for other than very weighty reasons. It is a matter of so great importance to me that they be trained to put duties first, giving pleasure a secondary place."

"But they are so good and industrious," said Violet. "And the sleighing is not likely to last long. It seldom does with us."

"They have been so closely confined to the house of late by the inclemency of the weather," he added.

"Yes, they shall go, for it will do them a great deal of good physically, I think, and health is, after all, of even more consequence for them than rapid advancement in their studies."

"I should think so, indeed," said Violet. "Now the next question is where shall we go?"

"That is a question for my wife to settle," returned the captain gallantly. "I shall be most happy to accompany her wherever she decides that she wishes to be taken."

"Thank you, sir. I want to see mamma, of course."

"Then we shall call at Ion, and perhaps may be able to persuade mother to join us in a longer ride."

"Oh, couldn't we hire an omnibus sleigh and ask them all to join us? It would just about hold the two families, I think."

"It is a trifle odd that the same idea had just occurred to me," he remarked pleasantly. "I will telephone at once to the town, and if I can engage a suitable sleigh, I will call to Ion and give our invitation."

The reply from the village was satisfactory—also that from Ion, given by Grandpa Dinsmore, who said he would venture to accept the invitation for all the family without waiting to consult them.

The captain reported to Violet then passed on into the apartments of his little daughters. He found them up and dressed, standing at the window of their sitting room looking out onto the grounds.

"Good morning, my darlings," he said.

"Oh, good morning, papa," they cried, turning and running into his outstretched arms to give and receive tenderest caresses.

"What were you looking at, my two daughters?" he asked presently.

"Oh, oh, the loveliest sight!" cried Lulu. "Do, papa, come and look," taking his hand and drawing him toward the window. "There, isn't it the loveliest?"

"Yes, I have seldom seen one finer," he answered.

"And the sun is shining so brightly, can't I take a walk with you today?" she asked, looking coaxingly up into his face.

"Why, my child, the walks and roads are sheeted with ice. You could not even stand, much less walk on them."

"I think I could, papa, if—if you'd only let me try. But, oh, don't looked troubled, for indeed, indeed, I'm not going to be naughty about it, though I have been shut up in the house for so long—except just riding in the closed carriage to church yesterday."

"Yes, and I know it has been hard for you," he said, smoothing her hair with a caressing hand.

Then sitting down, he drew her to one knee, Gracie to the other.

"How would my little girls like to be excused from lessons today and given, instead, a sleigh ride with papa, mamma, Max, and little Elsie?"

"Oh, ever so much, papa!" they cried, clapping their hands in delight. "How good of you to think of it!"

"'Specially for me, considering how very, very naughty I was only last week," added Lulu in a remorseful tone. "Papa, I really think I oughtn't to be allowed to go."

"And I really think I should not be deprived of the pleasure of having my eldest daughter with me on this first sleigh ride of the season," returned her father, drawing her into a closer embrace.

"And it would spoil all the fun for me to have you left at home, Lu," said Gracie.

"That must not be. We will all go, and I trust will have a pleasant time," the captain said, rising and taking a hand of each to lead them down to the breakfast room, for the bell was ringing.

At Ion the family was gathering about the table to partake of their morning meal. Walter waited rather impatiently till the blessing had been asked, then, with an entreating look at his mother, said, "Mamma, do you remember what you promised?"

"Yes, my son, but be patient a little longer. I see your grandfather has something to say."

"Something that Walter will be glad to hear, I have no doubt," remarked Mr. Dinsmore, giving the child a kindly look and smile. "Captain Raymond and I have had a little chat over the telephone this morning. He invites us all to join the Woodburn family in a sleigh ride. He is coming for us in an omnibus sleigh. I accepted for each and every one of you."

Zoe, Rosie, and Walter uttered simultaneous exclamations of delight, while the others looked well-pleased with the arrangement as well. "At what hour are we to expect the captain?" asked Mrs. Dinsmore.

"About ten."

"And where does he propose to take us?" inquired Zoe.

"I presume wherever the ladies of the party decide that they would like to go."

"Surely, papa, the gentlemen also should have a voice in that," his daughter said, sending him a bright, affectionate look from behind the coffee urn. "You, at least, in case the question is out to a vote."

"Not I more than the rest of you," he returned pleasantly. "But I have no doubt we would all enjoy the ride in any direction where the sleighing is good."

"I think it will prove fine on all the roads," remarked Edward. "And I presume everybody would enjoy riding over to Fairview, the Laurels, and the Oaks to call on our nearest relatives — perhaps to the Pines and Roselands also, to see the cousins there."

"That would be nice," said Zoe. "But don't you suppose they may be taking advantage of the sleighing opportunity as well as ourselves? Those families may be driving over here to call on us."

"Then, when we meet, the question will be who shall turn round and go back and who keep on," laughed Rosie.

"But to avoid such an unpleasant state of affairs we have only to ask and answer a few questions over the telephone," said Edward.

"Certainly," said his grandfather. "And we'll attend to it the first thing on leaving the table."

Everybody was interested, and presently all were gathered about the telephone while Edward, acting as the spokesman of the party, called to first one and then another of the households nearly related to them.

The answers came promptly, and it soon became evident that all were intending to avail themselves of the somewhat rare opportunity offered by the snow- and ice-covered roads, none planning to stay at home to receive calls. They would all visit Ion if the ladies there were likely to be in.

"Tell them," said Grandma Elsie, "to take their drives this morning, come to Ion in time for dinner, and spend the rest of the day and evening here. I shall be much pleased to have them all do so."

The messages went the rounds, everybody accepted the invitation, and Elsie's orders for the day to both cook and housekeeper were given accordingly for preparations for their guests.

The Woodburn party arrived in high spirits, and a sleigh containing the Fairview family drove up at the same time. They had room for one more and wanted mamma to occupy it, but the captain and Vi would not resign their claim. Evelyn and Lulu showed a strong desire to be together — so Evelyn was transferred to the Woodburn sleigh, and Zoe and Edward took the vacant seats in that from Fairview.

The two vehicles kept near together, and their occupants, the children especially, were very merry and lively. They talked of last year's holiday sports and indulged in pleasing anticipation in regard to what might be in store for them in those now drawing near.

"We had a fine at the Oaks, hadn't we, girls?" said Max, addressing Evelyn and Rosie.

"Yes," they replied. "But, I must say, a still better one at Woodburn."

"When are you and Lu going to invite us again?" asked Rosie.

"When papa gives permission," answered Max, sending a smiling, persuasive glance in his father's general direction.

"It is quite possible you may not have very long to wait for that, Max," came the kindly indulgent rejoinder from the captain.

"It is Rosie's turn this year," remarked Grandma Elsie. "Rosie's and Walter's and mine. I would like all of the young people of the connection — and as many of the older ones as we can make room for —

to come to Ion for the Christmas holidays, or at least the greater part of them. We will settle the particulars as to the time of coming and going later on. Captain, I would like you and Violet and all your children for the whole time."

"Thank you, mother. You are most kind, and I do not now see anything in the way of our acceptance of your invitation," he said. But then added with a playful look at Violet, "Unless my wife should object."

"If I should, mamma, you will receive my regrets in due season," laughed Violet.

The faces of the children were beaming with delight, and their young voices united in a chorus of pleasure and thanks to Grandma Elsie.

"I am glad you are all pleased with the idea," she said. "We will try to provide as great a variety of amusements as possible and shall be glad of any hints or suggestions from old or young in regard to anything new in that line."

"We will all try to help you, mamma," Violet said. "And none shall be jealous or envious if your party should far outshine ours of last year."

"And we have more than a month to get ready," remarked Rosie with satisfaction. "Oh, I'm so glad mamma has decided on it in such good season!"

"Hello!" cried Max, glancing back toward an intersecting road which they had just crossed. "Here they come!"

"Who?" asked several voices, while all turned their heads to see for themselves.

"The Oaks and the Roselands folks," answered Max. As he spoke, two large sleighs came swiftly up behind the rear of their own, while their occupants called out merry greetings and received a return in kind.

The wind had fallen, the cold was not intense, and they were so well protected against it by coats and robes of fur, that they scarcely felt it. They found the ride so thoroughly enjoyable that they kept it up through the whole morning, managing their return so that Ion was reached only a few minutes before the dinner hour.

Ion was a sort of headquarters for the entire family connection, and everybody seemed to feel perfectly at home. Grandma Elsie was a most hospitable hostess, and it was a very cheerful, jovial party that surrounded her well-spread table that day.

After dinner, while the older people conversed together in the parlors, the younger ones wandered at will through the house.

The girls were together in a small reception room, chatting about such matters as particularly interested them — their studies, sports, plans for the purchase or making of Christmas gifts, and what they hoped or desired to receive.

"I want jewelry," said Sydney Dinsmore. "I'd rather have that than anything else. But it must be handsome — a diamond pin, or ring, or earrings."

"Mamma says diamonds are quite unsuitable for young girls," said Rosie. "So I prefer pearls, and I'm rather in hopes that she may give me a set for Christmas."

"I'd rather have diamonds anyhow," persisted Sydney. "See Maud's new ring sent her by a rich old aunt of ours. I'm sure it looks lovely on her finger and shows off the beauty of her hand."

"Yes, I've been admiring it," said Lulu. "I thought I had not seen it before."

Maud held out her hand with evident pride and satisfaction, while all of the others gathered round her eager for a close inspection of the new, diamond ring.

They all admired it greatly, and Maud seemed much gratified.

"Yes," she said, "it certainly is a beauty and Chess says its must be worth a good deal. That center stone is quite large, you see, and there are six others in a circle around it."

"I should think you'd feel very rich," remarked Lulu. "I'd go fairly wild with delight if I had such a ring given me."

"Well, then, why not give your father a little bit of a hint that you'd like such a Christmas gift from him?" asked Sydney.

"I'm afraid it would cost too much," said Lulu. "And I wouldn't want papa to spend more on me than he could well afford."

"Why, he could afford it well enough!" exclaimed Maud. "Your father is very rich—worth his millions. I heard Cousin Horace say so not long ago. And he must know, of course."

Lulu looked much surprised. "Papa never talks of how much money he has," she said. "I never supposed it was more than about enough to keep us comfortable, but millions means a great deal, doesn't it?"

"I should say so, indeed! More than your mind or mine can grasp the idea of."

Lulu's eyes sparkled. "I'm ever so glad for papa!" she said. "He's just the right person to have a great deal of money, for he will be sure to make the very best use of it."

"And for the use of a part of it, that will be diamonds for you, won't it?" laughed Maud.

"I hope the captain will think so by the time she's grown up," remarked Rosie with a pleasant look at Lulu. "Or sooner, if they come to be thought to be suitable for girls of her age."

"That's nice of you, Rosie," Lulu said, flushing with pleasure. "And I hope you will get your pearls this Christmas."

"I join in both wishes," said Evelyn Leland. "I hope every one of you will receive a Christmas gift quite to her liking. But, oh, girls, don't you think it would be nice to give a good time to some of the poor people about us?"

"What poor people?" asked Sydney.

"Evelyn explained, "There are those Jones children that live not too far from Woodburn, for instance. Their mother's dead, and their father gets drunk and beats and abuses them. I'm sure they are altogether very, very forlorn."

"Oh, yes," cried Lulu. "It would be just splendid to give them a good time—nice things to eat and to wear and toys, too! I'll talk to papa about it, and he'll tell us what to give them and how to give it."

"And there must be a number of other families in the neighborhood probably quite as poor and forlorn," said Lora Howard. "Oh, I think it would be delightful to get them all together somewhere and surprise them with a Christmas tree loaded with nice things! Let's do it, girls. We all have some pocket money, and we can get our fathers and mothers to tell us how to use it to the best advantage and how to manage the giving."

"I haven't a bit more pocket money than I need to buy the presents I wish to give my own particular friends," objected Sydney.

"It's nice and right, too, I think, to give tokens of love to our dear ones," Evelyn said. "But we need not make them very expensive in order to give pleasure. Often they would prefer some simple thing that is the work of our own hands. Therefore, we would have something left for the poor and needy, whom the Bible teaches us we should care for and relieve to the best of our ability."

"Yes, I daresay you are right," returned Sydney. "But I shan't make any rash promises in regard to the matter."

CHAPTER SECOND

IN THE PARLOR THE older people were also conversing on somewhat similar topics—first discussing plans for the entertainment and gratification of their children and other young relatives during the approaching holidays, then of the needs of the poor of the neighborhood, and how to supply for them. After that they talked of the claims of home and foreign missions, the perils threatening their country from illiteracy, anarchy, heathenism, Mormonism, popery, infidelity—not omitting the danger from vast wealth accumulating in the hands of individuals and corporations. Also, they spoke of the heavy responsibility entailed by its possession.

They were both patriots and Christians, each quite anxious, first of all, for the advancement of Christ's kingdom upon earth, secondly for the welfare and prosperity of the dear land of their birth—the glorious old Union transmitted to them by their revolutionary fathers.

It was a personal question with each one: "How can I best use for the salvation of my country and the world the time, talents, influence, and money God has entrusted to my keeping?"

They acknowledged themselves stewards of God's bounty, and as such desired to be found faithful—neglecting neither the work nearest at hand nor that in far-distant lands where the people sat in great darkness and in the region and shadow of death, so that on them the "Son of righteousness might arise with healing in His wings."

It had been expected that the guests would stay at Ion till bedtime, but a thaw had set in and ice and snow were fast disappearing from the roads. Therefore, all departed for their homes directly after an early tea.

Lulu was very quiet during the homeward drive. Her thoughts were full of Maud's surprising assertion in regard to her father's wealth.

"I wonder if it is really so," she said to herself. "I'm tempted to ask papa, but he might not like it. And I wouldn't want to do anything to vex or trouble him—my dear, dear kind father!"

An excellent opportunity for a private chat with him was afforded her shortly after their arrival at home. The little ones were fretful, and Violet went to the nursery with them. Max hastened to his own room to finish a composition he was expected to hand to his father the next morning. Gracie, weary with the excitement of the day and the long morning drive, went directly to her bed, and Lulu, having seen her in it and left her there with a loving good night, the captain and Lulu presently found themselves the only occupants of the library.

Taking possession of a large easy chair, he said, "Come and sit on my knee and tell me how you have enjoyed your day, Lu," giving her a fond, fatherly smile.

"Very much indeed, papa," she answered, accepting his invitation, putting her arm round his neck, and laying her cheek to his.

His arm was round her waist. He drew her closer saying softly, "My dear, dear little daughter! I thought you were unusually quiet coming home. Is anything amiss with you?"

"Oh, no, papa! I've had a lovely time all day long. How kind you were to give us all a holiday and let us go along with the rest of you."

"Good to myself as well as to you, my darling. I could have had very little enjoyment if I had left you behind."

"Papa, it's so nice to have you love me so!" she said, kissing him with ardent affection. "Oh, I do hope I'll never, never be very naughty again!"

"I hope not, dear child," he responded, returning her affection. "I hope you feel ready to resume your studies tomorrow with diligence and painstaking?"

"Yes, papa, I think I do. It's almost a week since you have heard me recite—except the Sunday lesson yesterday."

"Yes," he said gravely. "It has been something of a loss to you in one way, but I trust a decided gain in another. Well, to change the subject, are you pleased with the prospect of spending the holidays at Ion?"

"Yes, papa, I think it will be lovely—almost as nice as having a party of our very own as we did last year."

"Possibly we may add that—a party here for a day or two—if Grandma Elsie does not use up all the holidays with hers," he said in a half-jesting tone and with a pleasant laugh.

"Oh, papa, do you really think we may?" she cried in delight. "Oh, you are just the kindest father!" giving him a hug.

He laughed at that, returning the hug with interest. "I suppose you and Eva and the rest were laying out plans for Christmas doings this afternoon?"

"Yes, papa, we were talking a good deal about games and tableaux and about the things we could buy or make for gifts for our friends, and what we would like to have given us."

She paused, hoping he would ask what she wanted from him, but he did not. He sat silently caressing her hair and cheek with his hand, seemingly lost deep in thought.

At length she asked half-hesitatingly, "Papa, are you very rich?"

"Rich?" he repeated, coming suddenly out of his reverie and looking smiling down into her eyes. "Yes. I have a sound constitution, excellent health, a delightful home, a wife and five children—each one of whom I esteem worth at least a million to me. I live in a Christian land," he went on with a graver tone. "I have the Bible with all its great and precious promises, the hope of a blessed eternity at God's right hand, and the knowledge that all my dear ones are traveling heavenward with me. Yes, I am a very rich man!"

"Yes, sir, but—I meant—have you a great deal of money?"

"Enough to provide all that is necessary for the comfort of my family and to gratify any reasonable desire on the part of my little girl. What is it you want, my darling?"

"Papa, I'm almost ashamed to tell you," she said, blushing and hanging her head. "But if I do, and you can't afford it, won't you please say so and not feel sorry about it? Because I wouldn't ever want you to spend money on me that you needed for yourself or some of the others."

"I am glad you are thoughtful for others as well as yourself, daughter," he said kindly. "But don't hesitate to tell me all that is in your heart. Nothing pleases me better than to have you and all my dear children do so."

"Thank you, my dear, dear papa. I don't mean ever to hide anything from you," she returned, giving him another hug and kiss, while her eyes sparkled and her cheek flushed with pleasure. "It's a diamond ring I'd like to have."

"A diamond ring?" he repeated in surprise. "What would my little girl do with such a thing as that?"

"Wear it, papa. Maud Dinsmore has such a beautiful one that a rich aunt sent her the other day," she went on eagerly. "There's a large diamond in the middle and little ones all around it, and it sparkles so and looks just lovely on her hand! We all admired it ever so much, and I said that I'd be wild with delight if I had one. Then Sydney said, 'Why not give your father a hint that you'd like one for Christmas?' I said that I was afraid you couldn't afford to give me anything that would cost so much, but Maud said I needn't be, for you were worth millions of money. Can you really afford to give it to me, papa? I'd like it better than anything else if you can, but if you can't, I don't want it," she concluded with a sigh as she crept closer into his embrace.

He did not speak for a moment, but though grave and thoughtful, his countenance was quite free from displeasure. When, at length, he spoke, his tones were very kind and affectionate.

"If I thought it would really be for my little girl's welfare and happiness in the end," he said, "I should not hesitate for a moment to gratify her in this wish of hers. But, daughter, the ornament you covet would be extremely unsuitable for one of your years. And I fear its possession would foster a love of finery that I do not wish to cultivate in you. I fear it would not be right and may hinder you in the race I trust you are running for the prize of eternal life.

"The Bible tells us we cannot serve both God and Mammon, cannot love Him and the world, too.

"'If any man love the world, the love of the Father is not in him.' God has entrusted me with a good deal of money, but I hold it as His steward, and 'it is required in stewards, that a man be found faithful.'"

"I don't know what you mean, papa," she said with a look and tone of keen disappointment.

"That I must use the Lord's money to do His work, daughter. A great deal of money is needed to help the advancement of His cause and kingdom in the hearts of individuals and in the world at large. There are millions of poor creatures in heathen lands who have never so much as heard of Jesus and His dying love. Even in our own favored country, there are thousands who are sunk in poverty, ignorance, and wretchedness. Money is needed to feed and clothe them, to send them teachers and preachers, and to build churches, schools, and colleges where they can be educated and fitted for happiness and usefulness.

"Suppose I had a thousand or even five thousand dollars to spare after supplying my family with all that is necessary for health, comfort, and happiness. Could my dear, eldest daughter be so selfish as to wish me to put it into a diamond ring for her at the expense of leaving some poor creature in want and misery, some poor heathen to die without the knowledge of Christ, or some soul to be lost that Jesus died to save?"

"Oh, no, no, papa!" she exclaimed, tears starting in her eyes. "I couldn't be so hard hearted. I couldn't bear to look at my ring if I knew it had cost so much to other people."

"No, I am sure you could not. And I believe you would find far more enjoyment and a far sweeter pleasure in selecting for me to use to benefit the money the ring might cost."

"Oh, papa, how nice, how delightful that would be if you would let me!" she cried joyously.

"I will," he said. "I have some thousands to divide among the various religious and benevolent groups, and I shall give a certain sum — perhaps as much as a thousand dollars — in the name of each of my three children who are old enough to understand these things. I will let each one of you select the cause, or causes, to which his or her share is to go."

"Which are the causes, papa?" she asked, her eyes sparkling with pleasure.

"There are home and foreign missions, the work among the freedmen and for the destitute in our own neighborhood, besides many others. We will read about these various causes and talk the matter over together and finally decide how many we can help and how much shall be given to each. Perhaps you may choose to support a little Indian girl in one of the mission schools, or some child in heathen lands, or a missionary who will go and teach them the way to heaven."

"Oh, I should love to do that!" she exclaimed. "It will be better than having a ring. Papa, how good you are to me! I am so glad God gave me such a father—one who tries always to teach me how to serve Him and to help me to be the right kind of a Christian."

"I want to help you in that, my darling," he said. "I think I could do you no greater kindness."

Just then Max came into the room, and his father called him to take a seat by his side, saying, "I am glad you have come, son, for I was about to speak to Lulu on a subject that concerns you quite as nearly."

"Yes, sir, I'll be glad to listen," replied Max, doing as directed.

The captain went on. "The Bible tells us, 'If any man have not the Spirit of Christ, he is none of His.' If we are like Jesus in spirit, we will love others and be ready to deny ourselves to do them good, especially to save their souls—for to that end He denied Himself even to the shameful and painful death of the cross.

"He says, 'If any man will come after me, let him deny himself, and take up his cross, and follow me . . . Whosoever doth not bear his cross, and come after Me, cannot be my disciple.'

"That is, we cannot be his disciples without doing something to bring sinners to Him that they may be saved—something that will cost us self-denial. It may be of our own ease, or of something we would like to do or have.

"And it must be done willingly, cheerfully, from love to the dear Master and the souls He died to save, and not as the way to earn heaven for ourselves.

"We cannot merit salvation, do what we will. We must take it as God's free, undeserved gift."

There was a moment of thoughtful silence, then Max said, "Papa, I think I am willing if I knew just what to do and how to do it. Can you tell me?"

"You have some money of your own every week. You can give what you will of that to help spread abroad the glad tidings of salvation. You can pray for others, and when a favorable opportunity offers, speak a word to lead them to Christ. Ask God to show you opportunities and give you grace and wisdom to use them. Try also, to live and act and speak, so that all who see and know you will take knowledge of you that you have been with Jesus and learned of Him."

"Papa," said Lulu, "won't you tell Max about the money you are going to give in our names?"

"No, I will let you have that pleasure," the captain answered with a kindly look and tone, and she eagerly availed herself of the permission.

Max was greatly pleased and Violet, who joined them just in time to hear what Lulu was saying, highly approved.

"But you will understand, children," the captain said, "that this involves your gaining a great deal of information on the subject of missions and other plans of benevolence. In order to help you in that, we will spend a short time each evening, when not prevented by company or some more important engagement, in reading and conversing on this topic."

"I wish I could earn some money to give," said Lulu. "I'd like to carve pretty things to sell, but who would buy them?"

"Papa might become a purchaser," her father said, stroking her hair and smiling kindly upon her.

"Or Mamma Vi," added her young stepmother.

"I have another offer to make you both," said the captain. "For every day that I find you obedient, pleasant-tempered, and industrious, I will give each of you twenty-five cents for your use in benevolent purposes."

"Thank you, papa," they both said, their eyes sparkling with pleasure. Max added, "That will be a dollar and seventy-five cents a week."

"Yes, and for every week that either one of you earns the quarter every day, I will add another to bring it up to two dollars."

"Oh, papa, how nice!" exclaimed Lulu. "I mean to try very hard, so that I may have enough to support a little Indian girl. And is Gracie to have the same?"

"Certainly, and I shall not be greatly surprised if Gracie's missionary box fills faster than either of the two others."

"I am almost sure it will," said Lulu, sobering a good deal. "And Max's will be next. But I mean to try ever so hard to be good."

"I am quite sure you do, dear child," her father responded in tender tones. "I know my little girl wants to improve, and I shall do all I can to help her."

"Papa, is that quarter a day good for conduct to be in addition to our usual pocket money?" inquired Max.

"Certainly, my son. Your pocket money is your own, to use for your pleasure or profit, except what you feel that you ought or desire to give of it, but the quarter is expressly and only for use in benevolent purposes."

"When may we begin to earn it, papa?"

"Tomorrow."

"I'm glad of that," said Lulu with satisfaction. "Because I woulk like very much to earn a good deal before Christmas."

Then she told of Evelyn's suggestions in regard to gifts for the poor in their immediate neighborhood.

"A very good idea," her father said. "And I think it may be carried out in a way to yield enjoyment to both givers and receivers."

"I hope it will be cold enough at Christmas time to make ice and snow for sleighing and sledding," Max remarked. "We boys have planned to have a good deal of fun for ourselves and the girls, too, if it is."

"You mean if there is sleighing and sledding," his father asked with an amused look. "It might be cold enough, yet the needed snow or ice be lacking."

"Why, yes, sir, to be sure, so it might!" Max returned, laughing good humoredly.

"What kind of fun is it you boys have planned for us girls?" asked Lulu.

"Never you mind," said Max. "You'll see when the time comes. The surprise will be half of it, you know, Lu."

"My dear, you seem to be a very wise and kind father," Violet remarked to her husband when they found themselves alone together after Max and Lulu had gone to their beds. "I highly approve of the plans you have just proposed to them. Though, of course, the approval of a silly young thing such as I must be a matter of small consequence," she added with a merry, laughing look up into his face.

"Young, but not silly," he returned with a lover-like look and smile. "I consider my wife's judgment worth a great deal, and I am highly gratified with her approval. I am extremely desirous," he went on more gravely, "to train my darlings to systematic benevolence, a willingness to deny themselves for the cause of Christ, and to take an interest in every branch of the work of the Church."

❧❧❧❧❧❧

CHAPTER THIRD

LULU'S FIRST THOUGHT upon awakening the next morning was of the talk of the previous evening with her father. He said she might have the pleasure of telling Gracie the good news in regard to the money to be earned by good conduct and that which was to be given by him in the name of each of his older children—also the particular cause or causes to which the money should go.

Eager to avail herself of the permission and to see Gracie's delight, she sprang from her bed, ran to the door between their sleeping rooms, which always stood open at night, and peeped cautiously in.

Gracie's head was still on her pillow, but at that instant she stirred, opened her eyes, and called out in a pleased tone, "Oh, Lu, so you are up first!" She spoke softly though, for fear of disturbing their father and Violet in the room beyond, as the door there being open also.

Lulu hurried to it and closed it gently, and then turning toward her sister, said, "Yes, but it's early, and you needn't get up just yet. I'm coming to creep in with you for a few minutes while I tell you something that I'm sure will please you."

She crept into Gracie's bed as she spoke, and they lay for a while clasped in each other's arms, Lulu talking very fast and Gracie listening and now and then putting in a word or two. She was quite as much pleased with what Lulu had to tell as the latter had anticipated.

"Oh, won't it be just lovely to have so much money to do good with!" she exclaimed when all had been told. "Haven't we got the very best and dearest father in the world? I don't believe, Lu, there's another half so dear and kind and nice. We ought to be ever such good children!"

"Yes, but I'm not," sighed Lulu. "Oh, Gracie, I'd give anything to be as good as you are!"

"Now, don't talk so, Lu. You make me feel like a hypocrite, because I'm not good," said Gracie.

"You are. At any rate, you're a great deal better than I am," asserted Lulu with warmth.

"You never disobey papa or get into a passion. And I don't think you love finery as I do. Gracie, I want that ring yet. Oh, I should like to have it ever so much! And I oughtn't to want it. It's very selfish, because to buy it would use up money that ought to go to send missionaries to the heathen or do good to some poor miserable creature. It's wrong for me to want it, because papa says it wouldn't be good for me. And if I were as good as I ought to be I'd never want anything he doesn't think best for me to have. But, oh, dear, how can I help it when I'm fond of pretty things?"

"Lu," said Gracie softly, "I do believe that if you ask the Lord Jesus to help you quit wanting it, He will. But if you didn't care for it, it wouldn't be denying yourself to do without it for the sake of the heathen or other poor souls."

"Maybe so, but I don't believe papa would let me have it even if I wouldn't consent to give it up and begged him ever so hard for it."

"No, I s'pose not, for he loves us too well to give us anything that he thinks will make it harder for us to love and serve God and go to heaven when we die."

"Yes, and of course that's the best way for people to love their children. It's time for me to get up now, but you'd better lie still a little longer."

With that Lulu slipped from the bed, ran back to her room, and kneeling down there, gave thanks for the sleep of the past night, for health and strength, a good home, her dear, kind father to take care of and provide for her and love her, and all her many, many comforts and blessings. Confessing her sins, she asked to be forgiven for Jesus' sake and to have strength given her to do all her duty that day—to be patient, obedient, industrious, kind, and helpful to others and willing to deny herself, especially in the matter of the ring she had been wishing for so ardently.

When the captain came into the apartments of his little daughters for a few minutes' chat before breakfast, as was his custom, he found them both neatly dressed and looking bright and happy.

"How are you, my darlings?" he asked, kissing them in turn, then seating himself and drawing them into his arms.

"I think we're both very well, papa," answered Lulu.

"Yes, indeed!" said Gracie. "I'm ever so glad of what Lu's been telling me 'bout the money you are going to give us if we're good and the choosing 'bout where the other shall go that you're going to give to help send missionaries to the heathen. Thank you for both, dear papa, but don't you think we ought to be good without being paid for it?"

"Yes, I certainly do, my little girl, but at the same time I want my children to have the luxury of being able to give something which they have, in some sense, earned for that purpose. I want you to learn in your own experience the truth of the words of the Lord Jesus, 'It is more blessed to give than to receive.'

"Now while you are so young, not capable of earning much in any other way, your proper business is the task of gaining knowledge and skill to fit you for future usefulness. I see no more fitting way than this for you to be furnished with money for religious and benevolent purposes."

"Papa," asked Lulu, "do you think it is never right for anybody to have diamonds or handsome jewelry of any kind?"

"I do not think it my business to judge in such matters for everybody," he answered, caressing her and smiling down tenderly into her eyes. "But I must judge for myself—applying the rules the Bible gives me—and to a great extent for my children also while they are so young."

"Not for Mamma Vi?" Lulu asked with some little hesitation.

"No, she is my wife, not my child, and she is old enough to judge for herself."

"She has a great deal of beautiful jewelry," remarked Lulu with an involuntary sigh. "And Grandma Elsie has still more. Rosie asked her once to show it to us children, and she did. Oh, she has the loveliest rings and whole sets of jewelry—pins and earrings to match—and chains and bracelets! I'm sure they must be worth a great deal of money. Rosie said they were, and I'm sure Grandma Elsie is a real Christian—a very, very good one and that Mamma Vi is, too."

"And I agree with you in that," was the emphatic reply. "But my daughter and I have nothing to do with deciding their duty for them in regard to this or other things. God does not require that of us— indeed, He forbids it. 'Judge not, that ye be not judged,' Jesus said.

"But I see plainly that my duty is as I explained it to you last evening. I thought then you were convinced that it would be selfish and wrong for you and me to spend a large sum for useless orna- ment that might otherwise be used for the good of our fellow creatures and the advancement of Christ's kingdom."

"Yes, papa, I was, and I'm trying and asking God to help me not to want the ring I asked you for. But I'm afraid it'll take me quite a while to quite stop wishing for it," she sighed.

"You will conquer at length, if you keep on trying and asking for help," he said, giving her a tender fatherly kiss.

"A good plan will be to fill your thoughts with other things," he went on. "Your lessons while in the schoolroom. After that you may find it pleasant to begin planning for Christmas gifts to be made or bought for those you love and others whom you would like to help. I shall give each of you— including Max—as much extra spending money as I did last year."

"Beside all that for benevolence, papa?" they asked in surprise and delight.

"Yes, what I provide you with for benevolence is something aside from your spending money, which you are at liberty to do with as you please, within certain bounds," he said, rising and taking a hand of each as the breakfast bell sounded out its summons to the morning meal.

Misconduct and poor recitations were alike very rare in the schoolroom at Woodburn. Neither found a place there today, so that the captain had only commendations to bestow, and they were heartily and gladly given.

The ice and snow had entirely disappeared and the roads were muddy—too muddy it was thought to make travel over them particularly agreeable. But the children obtained sufficient exercise in romping over the wide porches and trotting around the grounds on their ponies.

But in spite of the bad conditions of the roads, the Ion carriage drove over early in the afternoon, and Grandma Elsie, Mrs. Elsie Leland, Rosie, and Evelyn alighted from it. Everybody was delighted to see them and to hear that they would stay to tea.

"Oh, girls," said Lulu, "come up to my room and take off your things. I've something to tell you," and she looked so merry and happy that they felt quite sure it was something that pleased her greatly.

"I think I can guess what it is," laughed Rosie. "Your father has promised you the diamond ring you want so badly."

"No, it isn't that. You may have another guess, but I don't believe you could hit the right thing if you guess fifty or a hundred times."

"Then I sha'n't try. I give up. Don't you, Eva?"

"Yes, please tell us, Lu," said Evelyn.

Then Lulu, talking fast and eagerly, repeated to them what she had told Gracie in bed that morning.

"Oh, how nice!" Evelyn exclaimed. "How I should like to be in your place, Lu!"

"I think it's nice, too," Rosie said. "I'd like mamma or grandpa to do the same by me. But I'd want my pearls, too," she added, laughing. "Mamma's rich enough to give me them and do all she need do for missions and the poor beside."

"But so very much is needed," remarked Evelyn.

"I've read in some religious papers that if every church member would give but a small sum yearly, there would be enough," said Rosie. "And mamma gives hundreds and thousands of dollars, and grandpa gives a great deal, too. So I don't see that I ought to do without the set of pearls I've set my heart on. It isn't mamma's place to do other people's duty for them—in the way of giving any more than in other things."

Grandma Elsie and her older daughters were in Violet's boudoir.

"I had letters this morning from your brothers Harold and Herbert, Vi, and I have brought them with me to read to you," her mother said, taking the missives from her pocket.

"Thank you, mamma. I am always glad to hear what they write. Their letters are never dull or uninteresting," Violet replied. Her sister Elsie added, "They are always worth hearing, Lester and I think. What dear boys they are!"

"And quite as highly appreciated by my husband as by yours, Elsie," Violet said with a bright, happy look.

"They are a great blessing and comfort to their mother," Grandma Elsie remarked. "As indeed all my children are. Their letters are always a source of pleasure, but these even more so than most. They show that my college boys are greatly stirred up on the subject of missions at home and abroad—full of renewed zeal for the advancement of the Master's cause and kingdom."

She then read the letters that gave abundant evidence of the correctness of her estimate of the state of her sons' minds.

They were working as teachers in a mission Sunday school as Bible readers and tract distributors among the poor and degraded of the city where they were sojourning. They were doing good to bodies as well as souls—their mother supplying them with means for that purpose in addition to what she allowed them for pocket money. They were also exerting an influence for good among their fellow students.

They told of interesting meetings held for prayer and conference upon the things concerning the Kingdom, of renewed and higher consecration on the part of many who were already numbered among the Master's followers, and the conversion of others who had hitherto cared for none of these things.

The reading of the letters was followed by an earnest talk among the mother and her daughters in which Violet told of her husband's plan for giving through his children in addition to what he would give in other ways.

"What an excellent idea!" Grandma Elsie exclaimed, her eyes shining with pleasure. "I shall adopt that with my younger two children, as with all of you."

"Which is that last, mamma?" asked Violet.

"Letting each of you select a cause for a certain sum, which I shall give."

"Mamma, that is very nice and kind," remarked her daughter Elsie. "But we should give of our own means. Do you not think so?"

"You may do that in addition," her mother said. "I have seven children on earth—eight counting Zoe—and one in heaven. I shall give a thousand dollars in the name of each."

"Mamma, I for one fully appreciate your great kindness but think you would make a wiser choice of causes than we," said Violet, looking lovingly into her mother's eyes.

"I want to have the pleasure," her mother answered. "And I am reserving much the larger part of what I have to give for causes of my own selection. It has pleased the Lord to trust me with the stewardship of a good deal of the gold and silver which are His."

At that moment the little girls entered the room and Rosie, hurrying up to her mother, asked, "Mamma, have you heard—has Vi told you what the captain intends on doing? Do you know how he is going to reward his children for good behavior?"

"Yes, and I shall do the same by you and Walter."

"That's a dear, good mamma!" exclaimed Rosie with satisfaction. "I thought you would."

"And I intend to follow the captain's lead in another matter," Grandma Elsie went on, smiling pleasantly upon her young daughter. "That is in allowing each of my sons and daughters to select some good cause for me to give to in their names."

"That's nice, too," commented Rosie. "I like to be trusted in such things—as well as others," she added, laughing. "And I hope you'll trust me with quite a sum of money to give or spend just as I please!"

"Ah, my darling, you must not forget that your mother is only a steward," was the sweet-toned response given between a smile and a sigh. Grandma Elsie was not free from anxiety about this youngest daughter, who had some serious faults and had not yet entered the service of the Lord Jesus Christ.

"Evelyn, dear, you, too, as my pupil and a sort of adopted daughter, must share the reward of good behavior," she said with a tenderly affectionate look at the fatherless niece of her son-in-law.

Evelyn flushed with pleasure—more because of the loving look than the promise of reward. "Dear Grandma Elsie, how very kind and good you always are to me!" she exclaimed feelingly, her eyes filling with tears of love and gratitude.

"Dear child, whatever I have done for you has always been both a duty and a pleasure," Mrs. Travilla returned, taking the hand of the little girl who was standing by her side and pressed it affectionately in her own.

"Well, Eva," said Rosie lightly, "you can calculate to a cent what you'll have for benevolence, for you're sure to earn the quarter every day of your life."

"Not quite, Rosie," Evelyn answered in her gentle, refined tones. "I am liable to fall as well as others, and I may astonish both you and myself some day by behaving very ill indeed."

"I certainly should be astonished, Eva," laughed her Aunt Elsie. "I am quite sure it would be only under great provocation that you would be guilty of very bad behavior. And I'm equally certain that you will never find that at Ion."

"No," Evelyn said. "I have never received anything but the greatest kindness there."

"And you are so sweet tempered that you would never fly into a passion if you were treated ever so badly," remarked Lulu with an admiring, appreciative look at her friend, accompanied by a regretful sigh over her own infirmity of temper.

"Perhaps my faults lie in another direction. How much credit do people deserve for refraining from doing what they feel no temptation to do?" said Evelyn with an arch look and smile directed toward Lulu.

"And those that tease quick-tempered people and make them angry deserve at least half the blame," Rosie said softly in Lulu's ear, putting an arm affectionately about her as she spoke. "I don't mean to do so ever again, Lu, dear."

"I'm sure you don't, Rosie," returned Lulu in the same low key, her eyes shining. "It's ever so good of you to take part of the blame for my badness."

The visitors went away shortly after tea, Violet carried her babies off to bed, and the older three of the Woodburn children were left alone with their father.

They clustered about him. Gracie was on his knee, Lulu on one side, Max on the other, while their tongues ran fast on whatever subject happened to be uppermost in their thoughts. The captain encouraged them to talk freely, for he was most desirous to have their entire confidence in order that he might be the better able to correct wrong ideas and impressions, inculcate right views and motives, and lead them to tread the paths of rectitude, living noble, unselfish lives, serving God, and doing good to their fellow creatures.

Sensible questions were sure to be patiently answered and requests carefully considered and granted if both reasonable and within his power. Instruction was given in a way to make it interesting and agreeable. Reproof, if called for, was administered in a kind, fatherly manner that robbed it of its sting.

They talked of their sports, their pets, the books they were reading, the coming holidays, the enjoyment they were looking forward to at that time, and their plans for helping make it a happy time for others.

Evidently they were troubled with no doubt of their father's fond affection, or of the fact that he was their best earthly friend and wisest counselor.

"There are so many people I want to give to," said Lulu. "It will take ever so much thinking to know how to manage it."

"Yes, because we want to give things they'd like to have, and that we'll have money enough to buy, or time to make," said Gracie.

"Perhaps I can help you with your plans," said their father. "I think it would be well to make out a list of those to whom you wish to give. Then decide what amount to devote to each and what sort of thing would be likely to prove acceptable, yet not cost more than you have set apart for its purchase."

"Oh, what a nice plan, papa!" exclaimed Lulu. "We'll each make a list, sha'n't we?"

"Yes, if you choose. Max, my son, you may get out paper and pencils for us, and we will set to work at once. 'There is no time like the present' is a good motto in most cases."

Max hastened to obey and the lists were made out amid a good deal of pleasant chat—sometimes grave, sometimes merry.

"We don't have to put down all the names, papa, do we?" Gracie asked with an arch look and smile up into his face.

"No, we will except present company," he replied, stroking her hair caressingly and returning her smile with one full of tender, fatherly affection.

The names were all written down first, then came the task of deciding upon the gifts.

"We will take your lists in turn, beginning with Max's and ending with Gracie's," the captain said.

That part of the work required no little consultation between the three children. Papa's advice was asked in every instance and almost always decided the question. But, glancing over the lists when completed, he said, "I think, my dears, you have laid out too much work for yourselves."

"But I thought you always liked for us to be industrious, papa," said Lulu.

"Yes, daughter, but not overworked. I cannot have that, nor can I allow you to neglect your studies, omit needed exercise, or go without sufficient sleep to keep you in health."

"Papa, you always make taking good care of us the first thing," she said gratefully, nestling closer to him.

"Don't you know that's what fathers are for?" he said, smiling down on her. "My children were given to me to be taken care of, provided for, loved, and trained aright. A precious charge!" he added, looking from one to another with glistening eyes.

"Yes, sir, I know," she said, laying her head on his shoulder and slipping a hand into his. "Oh, but I'm glad and thankful that God gave me to you instead of to somebody else!"

"And Gracie and I are just as glad to belong to papa as you are," said Max.

Gracie added, "Yes, indeed!" as she held up her face for a kiss, which her father gave very heartily.

"But, papa, what are we to do about presents if we mustn't take time to make them?" asked Lulu.

"Make fewer and buy more."

"But maybe the money won't hold out."

"You will have to make it hold out by choosing less expensive articles or giving fewer gifts."

"We'll have to try hard to earn the quarter for good behavior every day, Lu," said Max.

"Yes, I mean to, but that won't help with Christmas gifts. It's only for benevolence, you know, Maxie."

"But what you give to the poor, simply because they are poor and needy, may be considered benevolence, I think," said their father.

"Oh, may it?" she exclaimed. "I'm glad of that! Papa, I—I haven't liked Dick very much since he chopped up the cradle I'd carved for Gracie's dolls, but I believe I want to give him a Christmas present. It will help me to forgive him and like him better. But I don't know what would please him best."

"Something to make a noise with," suggested Max. "A drum or trumpet, for instance."

"He'd make too much racket," she objected.

"How would a hatchet do?" asked Max with a waggish look and smile.

"Not at all. He isn't fit to be trusted with one," returned Lulu promptly. "Papa, what do you think would be a suitable present for him?"

"A book with bright pictures and short stories told very simply in words of one or two syllables. Dick is going to school and learning to read, and I think such a gift would be both enjoyable and useful to him."

"Yes, that'll be just right!" exclaimed Lulu. "Papa, you always do know best about everything."

"I hope you'll stick to that idea, Lu," laughed Max. "You seem to have only just found it out. Gracie and I have known it this long while, haven't we, Gracie?"

"Yes, indeed!" returned the little sister.

"And so have I," said Lulu, hanging her head and blushing. "Only sometimes I've forgotten it for a while. I hope I won't any more, dear papa," she added softly with a penitent look up into his face.

"I hope not, my darling," he responded in tender tones, caressing her hair and cheek with his hand. "And the past shall not be laid up against you."

"Papa, will you take us to the city as you did last year and let us choose ourselves the things we are going to give?" asked Max.

"I intend to do so," his father said. "Judging from the length of your lists, I think we will have to make several trips to accomplish it all. So we will make a beginning before long, when the weather has become settled. Perhaps the first pleasant day of next week, if you have all been both good and industrious about your lessons."

"Have we earned our quarters today, papa," asked Gracie.

"I think you are in a fair way to do so," he answered smiling. "But you still have a chance to lose them between now and you bedtime."

"It's just before we get into bed you'll give them to us, papa?" Lulu said inquiringly.

"I shall tell you at that time whether you have earned them, but I may sometimes only set the amount down to your credit and pay you the money in a lump at the end of the week."

"Yes, sir, we'll like that way just as well," they returned in chorus.

Violet had come in and taken possession of an easy chair on the farther side of the glowing grate.

Looking smilingly at the little group opposite. "I have a thought," she said lightly. "Who can guess what it is?"

"It's something nice about papa—how handsome he is and how good and kind," ventured Lulu.

"A very close guess, Lu," laughed Violet. "My thought was that the Woodburn children have as good and kind a father as could be found in all the length and breadth of the land."

"We know it, Mamma Vi. We all think so," cried the children.

But the captain shook his head saying, "Ah, my dear, flattery is not good for me. If you continue to dose me with it, who knows but I shall become as conceited and vain as a peacock?"

"Not a bit of danger of that!" she returned rather merrily. "But I do not consider the truth flattery."

"Suppose we change the subject," he said with a good-humored smile. "We have been making out lists of Christmas gifts and would like to have your opinion and advice in regard to some of them."

"You shall have both for what they are worth," she returned, taking the slips of paper Max handed her and glancing over them.

CHAPTER FOURTH

THE PARLOR AT ION, full of light and warmth, looked very pleasant and inviting this evening. The whole family—not so large now as it had been before Captain Raymond took his wife and children to a home of their own—were gathered there. There was Mr. Dinsmore and his wife—generally called Grandma Rose by the children—Grandma Elsie, her son Edward and his wife Zoe, and the two younger children—Rosie and Walter.

The ladies and Rosie were all knitting or crocheting. Mr. Dinsmore and Edward were playing chess, and Walter was deep in a story book.

"Zoe," said Rosie, breaking the present lull in the conversation, "do you know, has mamma told you, about her new plans for benevolence? Do you know how she is going to let us all help her in distributing her funds?"

"Us?" echoed Zoe inquiringly.

"Yes, all of her children, and that includes you, of course."

"Most assuredly it does," said Grandma Elsie, smiling tenderly upon her young daughter-in-law.

Zoe's eyes sparkled. "Thank you, mamma," she said with feeling. "I should be very sorry to be left out of the number. I am very proud of belonging there.

"But what about the new plans, Rosie? If mamma is willing, you should tell me now what they are."

"Quite willing," responded Grandma Elsie, and Rosie went on.

"You know mamma always gives thousands of dollars every year to home and foreign missions and other good causes, and she says that this time she will let each of us choose a cause for her to give a thousand to."

"I like that idea!" exclaimed Zoe. "Many thanks, mamma, for my share of the privilege. I shall choose to have my thousand go to help the mission schools in Utah. I feel so sorry for those poor Mormon women. The idea of having to share your husband with another woman, or maybe half a dozen or more is simply awful!"

"Yes, and that is only a small part of what Mormonism is responsible for," remarked Grandma Rose. "Think of the tyranny of their priesthood—interfering with the liberty of the people in every possible way. They claim the right to dictate what they shall read, where they shall send their children to school, with whom they shall trade, where they shall live. They even order them to break up their homes, make a forced sale of their property, and move into another state or territory at their own cost, or go on a mission."

"Their wicked doctrine and practice of what they call blood atonement, too," sighed Grandma Elsie.

"And the bitter hatred they inculcate toward the people and government of these United States," added Zoe. "Oh, I am sure both love of country and desire for advancement of Christ's cause and kingdom should lead us to do all we can to rescue Utah from Mormonism. Do you not think so, mamma?"

"I entirely agree with you and am well satisfied with your choice," Grandma Elsie replied.

"Perhaps I shall choose for mine to go there, too," said Rosie. "But I believe I'll take a little more time to consider the claims of other causes."

Walter closed his book and came to his mother's side. "Am I to have a share in it, too, mamma?" he asked.

"In selecting a cause for me to give to? Yes, my son."

"A thousand dollars?"

"Yes."

"Oh, that's good! I think I'll adopt an Indian boy—clothe and educate him."

"Adopt?" laughed Rosie. "A boy of ten talking about adopting somebody else!"

"Not to be a father to him, Rosie—except in the way of providing for him as fathers do for their children. Mamma knows what I mean."

"Yes, my boy, I do. And I highly approve. As a nation we have robbed the poor Indians and owe them a debt that I fear will never be paid."

"I mean to do my share toward paying it if I live to be a man," Walter said. "I'd like to begin now."

"I am very glad to hear it, my son," responded his mother.

"Would you prefer to have all your thousands go to pay that debt, mamma?" asked Rosie.

"No, child, not at all. As I have said, I highly approve of Zoe's choice, and I would send gospel tidings into the dark places of the earth—to the millions who have never heard the name of Jesus."

"There is another race to whom we owe reparation," remarked Mr. Dinsmore, leaning back in his chair and regarding the chess board with a rueful look. "There, Ned, my boy, I think you wouldn't have come off victor if my attention had not been called from the game by the talk of the ladies."

"Never mind, Grandpa. We'll take all the blame," laughed Rosie, jumping up to run and put her arms round his neck and give him a kiss.

He returned it, drew her to his knee, and went on with his remarks.

"You all know, of course, that I refer to the Negroes, who were forcibly torn from their own land and enslaved in this. We must educate and evangelize them—as a debt we owe them and also for the salvation of our country whose liberties will be greatly imperiled by their presence and possession of the elective franchise if they are left to both ignorance and vice."

"Grandpa, what do you mean by the elective franchise?" asked Walter, going to the side of the old gentleman's chair.

"The right to vote at elections, my son. You can see, can't you, what harm might come from it?"

"Yes, sir, they might help to put bad men into office. And bad men would be likely to make bad laws and favor rogues. Oh, yes, sir, I understand it perfectly!"

"Then perhaps you may want to help provide for the instruction of the colored race as well as the Indians, Walter?"

"Yes, sir, I think I would like to. I hope a thousand dollars will be enough to help the work for both."

"I think it will. I think your mother will be satisfied to have you divide in into two or more portions so that several good causes may receive some aid from it."

"Will you, mamma?" asked Walter, turning to her.

"Yes, I think it would perhaps be the wisest way."

"And besides," said Rosie, "mamma is going to give us young ones a chance to earn money for benevolence by paying us for good behavior. I know we ought to be good without other reward than that of a good conscience, but I'm quite delighted with the plan for all that."

"I, too," said Walter, looking greatly pleased. "Thank you, mamma dear. How much is it you're going to give us?"

"Twenty-five cents for every day on which I have no occasion to find fault with either your conduct or your recitations."

"A new idea, my daughter, isn't it?" queried Mr. Dinsmore.

"Yes, sir, and not original. I learned at Woodburn today that the captain was going to try the plan with his children. I trust it meets your approval? I might better have consulted you before announcing my intention to adopt it."

"That was not at all necessary," he returned pleasantly. "But I quite approve and trust you will find it works to your entire satisfaction."

"Speaking of helping the Negroes and thinking of the advice so often given, 'Do the work nearest at hand,' it strikes me that it would be well for us to begin with those in our own house and those who work the plantation," remarked Edward.

"I think they have never been neglected, Edward," said his grandfather. "A schoolhouse was provided for them years ago. Your mother pays a teacher to instruct them, visits the school frequently, and often gives religious instruction herself to the pupils there and to their parents when she visits them in their cabins. She also sees that they are taken care of in sickness, too, and that they do not suffer for the necessaries of life at any time."

"Yes, sir, that is all true,' returned Edward. "But I was only thinking of giving them some extra care, instructions, and gifts during the approaching holidays—say a Christmas tree loaded with not the substantials of life only, but some of the things that will give pleasure merely—finery for the women and girls, toys for the children.

"Meaning tobacco for the old folks and sweets for all, I suppose," added Zoe with both a sportive look and tone.

"Yes, my dear, that's about it," he said, smiling affectionately upon her.

"Oh, mamma, let us do it!" cried Rosie with enthusiasm. "Let's have a fine, big tree in their schoolroom and have them come there and get their gifts before we have ours here. We should get Vi and the captain to join us in it as the colored children from Woodburn attend school there, too."

"I am well pleased with the idea," replied her mother. "And I have little doubt that the captain and Vi will be also. But let us have your opinion, my dear father," she added, turning upon him with a look of mingled love and reverence.

"It certainly coincides with yours, daughter," Mr. Dinsmore answered. "And I move that Ned and Zoe be appointed a committee to find out the needs of the proposed recipients of our bounty and others being permitted to assist if they like."

The motion was carried by great acclamation, merry jesting and laughter followed, and in the midst of it all the door was thrown open and a visitor announced.

"Mr. Lilburn, ladies and gentlemen."

Grandma Elsie hastily laid aside her crocheting and hurried forward with both hands extended.

"Cousin Ronald! What a joyful surprise! Welcome, welcome to Ion!"

"Thanks, a thousand thanks, my fair kinswoman, my bonny leddy, my sweet Cousin Elsie," returned the old gentleman, taking the offered hands in his and imprinting a kiss upon the still round and blooming cheek. "I have ventured to come without previous announcement o' my intention or query about the inconvenience I might cause in your household arrangements, or —"

"No fear of that, sir," Mr. Dinsmore interrupted, offering his hand. "You know that you are, and always will be, a most welcome guest in my daughter's home. You have given a pleasant surprise and the fault will not be ours if we do not keep you all winter."

The others, from Mrs. Dinsmore down to Walter, followed suit with greetings no less joyous and cordial, for the old gentleman was a great favorite at Ion and with the whole connection.

He was presently installed in the easiest chair in the warmest corner and hospitably urged to take some refreshment.

But he declined, say he had had his supper in the village before driving over and wanted nothing more till morning.

He went on to account for his sudden appearance. He had been sojourning some hundreds of miles farther north and had not been well. His physician advised an immediate change to a more southerly climate, and he had set out at once for Ion, without waiting to let them know of his intentions. He felt sure of such a welcome as he had received.

"A month's warning could not have made you more welcome than you are, cousin," said his hostess.

The conversation that was broken in upon by Mr. Lilburn's arrival was not renewed that evening, but the subject was introduced again the next morning at the breakfast table, and some questions in regard to it were decided. All could not be, however, without consultation with the captain and Violet and with Lester and Elsie Leland.

Both families were speedily informed, through the telephone, of the arrival of Mr. Lilburn, and that afternoon saw them all gathered at Ion again to do him honor and to complete the arrangements for the holiday festivities.

During the intervening weeks there was a great deal of traveling back and forth between the three houses and to and from the city. Their plans involved a good deal of shopping on the part of both the older people and the children.

The latter were so full of pleasurable excitement that at times they found no little difficulty in giving proper attention to their studies. Such was especially the case with Rosie and Lulu, but both Grandma Elsie and Captain Raymond were quite firm, though in a kind and gentle way, in requiring tasks to be well learned before permission was given to lay them aside for more congenial employment.

Rosie besought her mother very urgently for her permission to sit up for an hour beyond her usual bedtime in order to make greater progress with her fancy work for Christmas, but her permission was not granted.

"No, my dear little daughter," Elsie said. "You need your usual amount of sleep to keep you in health, and I cannot have you deprived of it."

"But, mamma," returned Rosie a little impatiently, "I'm sure it couldn't do me any great amount of damage to try it a few times. I really think you might allow me to do so."

"My daughter must try to believe that her mother knows best," was the grave, though gently spoken rejoinder.

"I think it is a little hard, mamma," pouted Rosie. "I'm almost grown up, and it's so pleasant in the parlor where you are all talking together—especially now that Cousin Ronald is here—that it does seem too bad to have to run away from it all an hour before the older folks separate for the night. I'd feel it hard even if I wasn't wanting time for my fancy work for Christmas."

"A little girl with so foolish and unkind a mother as yours is certainly much to be pitied," Mrs. Travilla remarked in reply.

"Mamma, I did not mean that. I could never think or speak of you in that way," returned Rosie, blushing vividly and hanging her head.

"If you had overheard Lulu addressing the remarks to her father that you have just made to me, would you have taken them as evidence of her confidence in his wisdom and love for her?" asked her mother. Rosie was obliged to acknowledge that she would not.

"Please forgive me, mamma," she said penitently. "I'll not talk so again. I haven't earned my quarter for good behavior today. I'm quite aware of that."

"No, my child, I am sorry to have to say you have not," sighed her mother.

It was one afternoon in the second week after Mr. Lilburn's arrival that this conversation between Rosie and her mother was held.

At the same hour Max and Lulu were both in their workroom at home, busily carving. Since their dismissal from that morning's tasks, they had spent every moment of time at that work, except what had necessarily been given to the eating of their dinner.

Presently their father came in.

"You are very industrious, my darlings," he said in a pleasant tone. "But how much exercise have you taken in the open air today?"

"Not any yet, papa," answered Max.

"Then it must be attended to at once by both of you."

"Oh, papa, let me keep on at this just a little longer," pleaded Lulu.

"No, daughter, not another minute. These winter days are short. The sun will soon set and outdoor exercise will not do you half so much good after sundown as before. Put on your hats and coats, and we will have a brisk walk together. The roads are quite dry now, and I think we will find it enjoyable."

The cloud that had begun to gather on Lulu's brow at the refusal to her request vanished with the words of invitation to walk with papa, for to do so was one of her dearest delights.

Both she and Max obeyed the order with cheerful alacrity, and presently the three sallied forth together to return in time for tea in good spirits and with fine appetites for their meal—the children both rosy and merry.

Violet was teaching Lulu to crochet, and the little girl had become much interested in her work. When the hour for bedtime came she did not want to give it up, and like Rosie begged for permission to stay up for another hour.

"No, dear child," her father said. "It is quite important that little ones like you should keep to regular hours—early hours, too, for going to rest."

"Then may I get up sooner in the mornings while I'm so busy?" she asked coaxingly.

"If you find yourself unable to sleep, not otherwise. My little girl's health is of far more importance than the making of the most beautiful Christmas gifts," he added with a tender caress.

"And I sha'n't forget this time that papa knows best," she said in a cherry tone, giving him a hug.

He returned it. "I think tomorrow is likely to be a pleasant day," he said. "And if so I hope to take my wife and children to the city for some more of the shopping you all seem to find so necessary and delightful just now. Your Aunt Elsie and Evelyn are going, too, so that you can probably have your friend's help in selecting the articles you wish to buy."

"Oh, how delightful!" she exclaimed. "I ought to be a good girl with such a kind father—always planning something to give me pleasure."

"You enjoy such expeditions, don't you, Lu?" queried Violet.

"Yes, indeed, Mamma Vi, and I hope papa will take me several times. I want to select my gift for Rosie tomorrow with Eva to help me. And I'd like Rosie to go with me another time to help me choose one for Evelyn."

"I think I shall be able to gratify you in that. And to give you more time for Christmas work, I will release you from the task of taking care of your own rooms, till after the holidays. I will have them attended to by one of the servants," said the captain. "But now bid goodnight and go to your bed."

"Oh, thank you, dear papa," she cried joyously and obeyed at once without a murmur.

The weather the next day was favorable, and the shopping a decided success. The ladies and little girls returned somewhat weary with their exertions but in fine spirits. Lulu was feeling particularly happy over a present for Rosie, which everyone thought was sure to be acceptable.

A few days later her father took her and Rosie together, Evelyn being left out of the party in order that her present might be selected without her knowledge.

Indeed, in the afternoon of every pleasant day, from that to the one before Christmas, the Woodburn carriage might have been seen driving to and from the city. And on almost every occasion, Lulu was one of the occupants.

But on the twenty-third she preferred to stay behind—so much that she wanted a share in what was going on at or near home. First there was the trimmings with evergreens of several rooms in the mansion, then of the schoolhouse for the poor whites of the neighborhood. Captain Raymond had caused it to be built on a corner of his estate— paying a teacher that the children might be instructed without cost to the parents.

A fine Christmas tree was set up in it and another in the schoolhouse for the servants at Ion.

The children of the servants employed on the Fairview estate attended there also and were to have a share in the entertainment provided for those of Woodburn and Ion. The children of the three families united in the work of ornamenting first one building, then the other. They found it great sport and flattered themselves that they were of great assistance, though the older people who were overseeing matters and the servants acting under their direction were perhaps of a different opinion. Yet the sight of the enjoyment of the little folks more than atoned for the slight inconvenience of having them about.

Christmas came on Wednesday that year, and the holidays had begun for them all the Friday before. Lessons would not be taken up again till after New Year's Day.

It had been decided at Woodburn that they would not go to Ion till Christmas morning, as they all preferred to celebrate Christmas Eve at home. The children were going to hang up their stockings, but had not been told that they would have a tree or any gifts. They thought and had said to each other that perhaps papa might think the money he had given them to spend and to give, and the privilege of selecting causes for his benevolence, was enough from him. But the friends at Ion and Fairview always had remembered them and most likely would do so again.

"Still, they may not," Lulu added with a slight sigh when she talked the matter over with Max and Gracie that morning for the last time. "They are all giving more than usual to missions and disabled ministers and poor folks, and I don't know what else. But it's real fun to give to the poor around here—I mean, it will be to help put things on the trees and then see how pleased they'll all be when they get 'em. At least, I do suppose they will. Don't you, Max?"

I shall be very much surprised if they're not," he assented. "Though I begin to find out that 'it's more blessed to give than to receive.' And yet for all that, if I get some nice presents tonight or tomorrow, I—well, I sha'n't be at all sorry," he added with a laugh.

"Max," said Lulu reflectively, "you knew about the Christmas tree beforehand last year. Hasn't papa told you whether we're to have one this time or not?"

"No, not a word. And he tells me almost always what he intends to have done about the place," the boy went on with a look of pride in the confidence reposed in him. "I'm afraid it's pretty good evidence that we're not to have one."

For a moment Gracie looked sorely disappointed. Then, brightening, she said, "But I'm most sure that papa and mamma won't let us go without any presents at all. They love us a great deal and will be sure to remember us with a little bit of something."

"Anyway, it's nice that we have something for them," remarked Lulu cheerily. "Papa helped us choose Mamma Vi's, and she advised us what to make for papa, so I'm pretty sure they'll both be quite pleased."

It was while waiting for their father to take them to the schoolhouse that they had this talk. But it was brought to a conclusion by his voice summoning them to get into the carriage.

"There is no time to lose, my darlings," he said. "It is likely to take all the morning to trim the two rooms and trees."

CHAPTER FIFTH

GRANDMA ELSIE'S college boys, Harold and Herbert Travilla, had come home for the holidays, arriving the latter part of the previous week. This morning they had come over to Woodburn very soon after breakfast, "to have a chat with Vi while they could catch her alone," they said. "For with all the company that was to be entertained at Ion they might not have so good a chance again."

They stood with her at the window watching the carriage as it drove away with the captain and his children. It had hardly reached the gate leading into the high road when Harold turned to his sister with the remark, "Well, Vi, we've had quite a satisfactory talk—now for action. As I overheard the captain say to the children, 'there's no time to lose.'"

"No, we will begin at once," returned Violet, leading the way to the large room where the Christmas tree had been set up last year.

A few of the servant men were carrying in its counterpart at one door as Violet and her brothers entered at the other.

"Ah, that's a fine tree, Jack!" she said, addressing one of them. "The captain selected it, I suppose?"

"Yes, Miss Wi'let, de cap'n done say dis hyar one was for de Woodburn chillen, an' we's to watch an' fotch 'em in soon's dey's clar gone out ob sight."

"Yes," she said. "We want to give them a pleasant surprise. I think they are doubtful as to whether their father intends that they shall have a tree this year," she added, aside to her brothers.

"Then the surprise will be the greater," Harold returned. "That's half the fun. I suppose they might be pretty certain of the tree and would be surprised only by the nature of the gifts."

"They will have a goodly supply of those," Violet said with a pleased look, glancing in the direction of a table heaped with packages of various sizes and shapes. "Do you know, boys, when Christmas time comes around I always feel glad I married a man with children. It's such a dear delight to lay plans for their enjoyment and to carry them out."

"Just like you, Vi," said Herbert. "I like to hear you talk that way, but you have your own two."

"Yes, but even Elsie is hardly old enough yet to care very much for such things."

The tree now in place, the work of trimming it began.

"It's very good of you two boys to come here and help me instead of joining in the fun they are doubtless having at the schoolhouse," remarked Violet, as she handed a glittering fairy to Harold who was mounted upon a step ladder along side the tree. "There, I think that will look well perched on that topmost bough."

"Our tastes agree," he said, fastening the fairy in the designated spot.

"Yes, I think Herbie and I are entitled to any amount of gratitude on your part for the great self-denial we are practicing and the wonderful exertions we shall put forth in carrying out your wishes and directions in regard to this most difficult and irksome of business."

"And the fine phrase and well-turned periods contained in the remarks bestowed upon your unsophisticated country sister," laughed Violet.

"Of course, they must not be forgotten in the reckoning up of your causes for gratitude. Ah, Vi, how my heart goes out in pity and sympathy for you when I reflect that you not only never have shared in the inestimable privileges and delights of college-boy life, but are, in the very nature of things, forever barred from participation in them!"

"I certainly appreciate your feelings upon the subject," she said with mock gravity. "But I would advise that for the present you forget them and give your undivided attention to the business at hand. That second fairy does not maintain a very graceful attitude, brother."

"True enough," he said, promptly altering its position. "There, how's that for high?"

"Is it possible I hear such slang from the finely educated tongue of a college boy?" she exclaimed with a gesture of astonishment and dismay.

"She's high enough," said Herbert, gazing quite scrutinizingly at the fairy. "But there'd better be more work and less talk if we are to get through before the captain and his party come home."

"Herbert, when Mrs. Raymond and I have reached your venerable age you may expect to find us as sedate and industrious as you are now," remarked Harold, proceeding to hang upon the tree various ornaments as Herbert handed them to him.

"And in Harold's case due allowance must be made for the exuberance of spirits of a boy just let out of school," added Violet.

"And in your case, my dear madam, for what? Is it a youthful flow of spirits consequent upon a temporary release from the heavy responsibilities of wifehood and motherhood?"

"Very temporary," laughed Violet. "My husband will be home again in a few hours, and the call to attend my babies may come at any moment."

"I daresay if the captain had consulted only his own inclination he would be here now, overseeing his job," remarked Harold interrogatively.

"Yes," replied Violet. "But he thought his duty called him to the other places. And I think my good husband never fails to go where duty calls. We talked it over and concluded that the best plan we could hit upon was for me to stay at home and see to this work, while he should take his children and assist at the decoration of the schoolhouses."

"To secure for you an opportunity to prepare a pleasant surprise for them," supplemented Harold.

Their work was finished, its results surveyed with satisfaction, and the door of the room closed and locked upon it before the return of Captain Raymond and his merry and happy little flock.

Dinner filled up the greater part of the interval between their homecoming and return to the school on the corner of the estate to witness the distribution of gifts to the poor of the neighborhood. And by a little management on the parts of their father, Violet, and her brothers, they were kept from the vicinity of the room where the Christmas tree stood and got no hint of its existence.

Their thoughts were full of the doings of the morning and the coming event of the afternoon, and their tongues ran fast on the two subjects. Their father had to remind them once or twice that older people must be allowed a chance to talk as well as themselves, but his tone was not stern. The slight reproof, though sufficient to produce the desired effect, threw no damper upon their youthful spirits.

They were in the carriage again soon after leaving the table, Violet with them this time, and Harold and Herbert riding on horseback along side of the vehicle, for they desired a share in witnessing the bestowal of the gifts.

They found teacher and pupils there before them— every face bright with pleasurable anticipation.

The Jones children, whose mother had died the year before and who continued to find a good friend in Captain Raymond, were among the number.

Grandma Elsie, Zoe, Rosie, Walter, and Evelyn Leland arrived in a body soon after the Woodburn family, and then the exercises began.

The captain offered a short prayer and made a little address appropriate to the occasion. The teacher and scholars sang a hymn, a Christmas carol. Then the tree was unveiled amid murmurs of admiration and delight, and the distribution of the gifts began.

Every child received a suit of warm, comfortable clothes, a book, a bag of candy, a sandwich or two, some cakes, and fruit.

The tree was hung with rosy-cheeked apples, oranges, bananas, bunches of grapes, and strings of popcorn. There were bright tinsel ornaments, too, and a goodly array of brightly dressed paper dolls, mostly Gracie's contribution.

She had given up all her store for the gratification of the children.

"I've had such good times myself, playing with them and dressing them, that I do believe the poor children that don't have half the pleasures I do will enjoy them, too, and I can do very well without," she said to Lulu on deciding to make the sacrifice.

So she told her father they were not to be used merely as a temporary ornament for the tree, but to be given away to some of the younger girls attending the school.

They, along with other pretty things, were taken from the tree and presented last of all, and the delight manifested by the recipients more than made amends to Gracie for her self-denial.

From the Woodburn schoolhouse family and friends all repaired to the one at Ion, and a similar scene was enacted there. The exercises and the gifts to the children were very nearly the same, but there were older people—house servants and laborers on the estates—to whom were given more substantial gifts in money and provisions for the support of their families.

The afternoon was waning when the Raymonds again entered their family carriage and the captain gave the order, "Home to Woodburn."

And now the children began to think of the home celebration of Christmas Eve and to renew their wonderings as to what arrangements might have been made for their own enjoyment upon their return.

"Tired, children?" queried their father, putting an arm round Gracie as she leaned confidingly up against him and smiling affectionately upon them all.

"Oh, no, sir, not at all!" replied Max, quickly straightening himself with the air of one who had no thought of fatigue.

"Not at all, papa," echoed Lulu.

"Only just a little bit, papa," Gracie said with a cheerful tone. "We have had such a nice day."

"Giving pleasure to others," he remarked, patting the rosy cheek resting against his shoulder. "There is nothing more enjoyable. The little girls were very glad to get your dollies."

"Yes, sir. I'm so glad I gave them."

The carriage stopped. They were at their own door. In another minute they had all alighted, and the children were following their father and Violet into the house.

A Newfoundland dog, a magnificent specimen of his breed, met them almost at the threshold.

"Oh!" cried the children in excited chorus. "Where did he come from? Whose dog is he?"

"Max's—a Christmas gift from papa," answered the captain.

"Oh!" exclaimed Max, his face sparkling all over with delight. "What a splendid fellow! Papa, thank you ever so much! You couldn't have given me a more acceptable present."

"Ah? I'm glad you like him. But come into the library, all of you, for a moment. It is not quite tea time yet."

The captain led the way as he spoke, everybody else following.

"Howdy do? Where you been?" called out a rather harsh voice, and sending a surprised, inquiring glance about in search of the speaker, the children presently spied a cage with a parrot in it. It was an African parrot—gray with a scarlet tail.

"Polly wants a cracker!" screamed the bird. "Time for breakfast, Lu! Where you been?"

"How will Polly suit you for a Christmas gift, Lulu?" asked the captain, smiling down into the flushed, delighted face of his eldest daughter.

"Oh, papa, is it for me?" she cried breathlessly.

"Yes, if you want it; though I fear she may prove a rather troublesome pet. Here is Gracie's gift from papa," he added, pointing to a beautiful Maltese kitten curled upon the rug before the fire. "We mustn't let Max's big gift swallow your little one. I trust that in time we can teach them to be friends."

Gracie loved kittens and was no less delighted with her present than her brother and sister with theirs.

"Oh, the pretty pet!" she exclaimed, dropping down on the rug beside it and gently stroking its soft fur. "I'd like to take you on my lap, pretty puss, but you're fast asleep, and I won't wake you."

"That is right, my darling. I am glad to see my little girl thoughtful of the comfort of even a cat," her father said, bending down to stroke Gracie's hair with a tenderly caressing hand.

"I s'pose they have feelings as well as other folks, papa," she said, smiling up affectionately into his face. "I mean to be very kind to this pretty puss. And, oh, I'm ever so much obliged to you for her!"

His reply was prevented by a sudden, loud bark from the dog as he spied pussy on the rug.

"Turn him out into the hall, Max," the captain said, hastily stepping in between dog and cat. "Don't be alarmed for your pet, Gracie. He shall not be permitted to harm her."

"Nor my Polly either, shall he, papa?" asked Lulu, who was trying to make acquaintance with her new possession.

"No, certainly not. But take care of your fingers, daughter. She may snap at them and give you a bite that you will remember for a long while. Now go and get yourselves ready for tea. It is almost time for the bell to ring."

The children made haste to obey. The captain and Violet lingered behind for a moment.

"How pleased they are!" she said with a joyous look up into her husband's face. "It's a perfect treat to witness their delight on such occasions. I can hardly wait to show them the tree with all its treasures."

"Dear wife, your affection for my darlings is a wellspring of joy for me," he said with tender look and smile. "And theirs for you is no less so. I am sure you have completely won their hearts."

"You make me very happy," she responded, her eyes shining with joy and love. "But there! Do you hear little Elsie calling for papa and mamma?"

The faces that surrounded the tea table that evening were very bright, though the children had no expectation of the treat in store for them. Each had had a present from papa, and that was almost more than they had ventured to hope for.

But they were in merry spirits, looking forward to a time of rare enjoyment in spending the Christmas holidays with Grandma Elsie at Ion.

"We'll be glad to go," remarked Lulu. "And then glad to come back to our own dear home."

"So you will be twice glad," said her father.

"Yes, that is just the way I feel about it," Violet said. "Mamma's house will always be home to me—a dear home. Yet my husband's is doubly so."

"It should, seeing that it is quite as much yours as his," he said with a gratified smile. "Well, my darling, I see we have all finished eating. Shall we go now?"

"Yes, sir, if you please. Our little girls will want to take another peep at their new pets," she said, rising and slipping her hand into his arm.

They passed out of the room together, the children following close behind.

But on reaching the hall, instead of going into the library they turned toward the parlor on the other side of it, in which, as the children well remembered, last year's Christmas tree had been set up.

The captain threw open the door and there stood a larger and finer tree blazing with lights from many tapers and colored lamps and loaded with many beautiful things.

"Oh! Oh! What a beauty! What a splendid tree!" cried the children, dancing about and clapping their hands in delight. "And we didn't know we were to have any at all. Mamma Vi, you must have had it set up and trimmed it while we were gone this morning. Didn't you? Oh, thank you ever so much!"

"Your father provided it and your thanks are due to him far more than to me," Violet replied with a smiling glance in his direction.

At that they crowded about him, Max putting a hand affectionately into his and thanking him with hearty words of appreciation, while the little girls hugged and kissed him to his heart's content.

The servants had gathered about the door, little Elsie's mammy among them with her nursling in her arms.

"Oh, pretty, pretty!" shouted the little one, clapping her hands in an ecstasy of delight. "Let Elsie down, mammy."

"Come to papa," the captain said, and taking her to the tree and all around it, he pointed out all the pretty things.

"What would you like to have?" he asked. "What shall papa give you off this beautiful tree?"

"Dolly," she said, reaching for a lovely bisque doll in a tiny chair attached to one of the lower branches.

"You shall have it. It was put there on purpose for papa's baby girl," he said, taking it up carefully and putting it into her arms. "Now let us see what we can find for mamma and your brother and sisters."

His gift to Violet was some beautiful lace selected with the help of her mother. He had contrived to add it to the adornments of the tree without her knowledge. She was greatly pleased when he detached it and handed it to her.

Max was delighted to receive a magic lantern and a Sleight of Hand outfit, Lulu a game of Lawn and Parlor Ring Toss and a handsome toiletries case. Gracie had the same and beside a brass bedstead for her dolls with mattress and pillows and a large and complete assortment of everything needed for making and dressing paper dolls. That last was from Lulu.

There were books, periodicals, a typewriter, and games to be shared by all three, besides other less important gifts from one to the other and from outside friends. The servants, too, were remembered with gifts suited to their needs and tastes and there were fruits and confections for all.

Examining their own and each other's gifts, peeping into the new books, trying the new games with papa and mamma helping, the children found the evening pass very quickly and delightfully.

"We were going to hang up our stockings," Gracie remarked as the good nights were being said. "But we've had so many nice things already tonight that it does seem as if we oughtn't to do it."

"Oh, yes, do hang them up," said their father laughingly. "Santa Claus won't feel obliged to put anything into them."

"Perhaps if he doesn't find them hanging up, he may feel hurt at your low opinion of his generosity," laughed Violet.

"Oh, I wouldn't like to hurt his feelings, 'cause I'm sure he must be a very nice old fellow," returned the little girl with an arch look and smile. "So I'll hang mine up."

"And I, mine," said Lulu, twining her arms about her father's neck and looking up lovingly into his face. "For I know he's nice and generous and good as gold, though he isn't old or the sort of person to be called a fellow."

"Indeed! One might infer that you were quite well acquainted with him," laughed the captain, giving her a hug and a kiss. "Yes, hang it up. And, Max, if you don't feel it beneath the dignity of a lad of your size, there will be no harm in your trying the same experiment."

"I'm ashamed to think of it, sir, only because I've already had so much," said Max.

"But you are always safe in following your father's advice," remarked Violet.

"Oh, yes, I know that, and I'll do it, Mamma Vi," returned the boy with ill-concealed satisfaction.

"Now, all three of you get to bed and to sleep as soon as you can in order to give the old fellow a chance to pay his visit," said the captain. "I have always understood that he never does so till all the children in the house are asleep. I'll go in to kiss my little girls goodnight after they are snug in bed, but we will reserve our talk till morning."

"Yes, papa, we will," they said and hastened away to do his bidding.

At Ion, too, there was a beautiful Christmas tree, bearing fruit not very dissimilar to that of the one at

Woodburn. It had been the occasion of much mirth and rejoicing on the part of the children and pleasure to the older people. The gifts had been apportioned, those of the servants bestowed and carried away, but most of those belonging to the family and all the ornaments were left upon it that the guests of tomorrow night might be treated to the spectacle of its beauty.

CHAPTER SIXTH

CAPTAIN RAYMOND, going into Gracie's room to fulfill his promise to give her a goodnight kiss, found Lulu there also—the two clasped in each other's arms.

"We thought we'd sleep together tonight, papa," said Lulu. "If you're willing."

"I have no objection," he answered. "Gracie was a little afraid to receive Santa Claus alone, was she?" looking down at them with a humorous smile as he stood by the bedside.

"Oh, no, papa! I'm pretty sure I know who he is, and I'm not one bit afraid of him," answered the little girl with a merry laugh, catching his hand and carrying it to her lips.

"Ah! Then it was Lulu who was afraid, was it?"

"Oh, no, sir! Lu's never afraid of anything."

"Indeed, you seem to have a high opinion of her courage! You need never, either of you, be afraid or ashamed of anything but sin, my darlings," he added more gravely. "If you are God's children nothing can harm you. He will watch over us through the dark and silent night while we are wrapped in slumber. 'Behold He that keepeth Israel shall neither slumber or sleep.'"

"I'm so glad the Bible tells us that, papa," she said. "But I'm glad, too, that you sleep in the next room and have the door open always at night, so that if I should want you, you could easily hear me call and come to me."

"Yes," he said. "Neither of my little girls need ever hesitate for a moment to call for their father if they are ill or troubled in any way.

"Ah, I see the stockings hanging on each side of the fireplace. But how is Santa to tell which is Lulu's and which is Gracie's?"

"Why we never thought of that!" exclaimed Lulu, laughing. "But mine's a little bit larger, and it's red. Gracie's is blue. Don't you suppose, papa, that he'll be smart enough to guess which is which?"

"I think it is likely, but you will have to take the risk," replied her father. Then with a goodnight kiss, he left them to their slumber.

Day was faintly dawning when Lulu awoke. "Merry Christmas, Gracie!" she whispered in her sister's ear. "I'm going to get our stockings and see if there is anything in 'em." With a bound, she was out on the floor and stealing across it to the fireplace with care to make no noise.

She could not refrain, however, from a delighted "Oh!" as she laid hold of the stockings and felt that they were stuffed full of something.

"Did he come? Is there something in 'em?" whispered Gracie as Lulu came back to the bedside.

"Yes, yes, indeed! They're just as full as they can be! I've brought 'em. Here's yours," putting it into Gracie's hands and getting into bed again. "Let's pull the things out and feel what they are, though we can't see much till it gets lighter."

"Yes, let's," said Gracie. "I couldn't bear to wait."

They thought they were keeping very quiet, but Lulu's "Oh!" had awakened her father and Violet.

They were lying quietly listening and laughing softly to themselves.

There was a rustle of paper, then Gracie's voice in a loud whisper, "Oh, another dolly for me! And I just know it's lovely! I can feel it's hair, and it's dress. It's all dressed!"

Then Lulu's, "A potato! Just a horrid, raw Irish potato! What do I want with that?"

"And I've got one, too!" from Gracie. "Oh, well, I s'pose that was to fill up. Maybe there's something nice lower down."

"A sweet potato or a parsnip or something of that kind in mine," said Lulu, some slight vexation in her tone. "Oh, well, I've had so many nice things, and this is only for fun."

"And here are some candies in mine," said Gracie. "Haven't you got some?"

"Yes, oh, yes! And nuts and raisins. I'd like to taste them, but I think we'd better leave them till after breakfast. I'm pretty sure papa would say so."

"Yes, 'course he would, so we'll wait."

"Good, obedient children, aren't they, Vi?" the captain said in a gratified whisper to Violet.

"Very! I'm proud of them," she responded.

It was growing light, and Lulu, taking up the despised potato, examined it more critically. Presently she uttered an exclamation. "Oh, Gracie, see! It opens and there's something inside!"

The captain and Violet listened intently for what might come next.

"More candies and—something wrapped up in soft paper. Oh, Gracie! It's a lovely little pin!"

"Oh, oh, how pretty!" cried Gracie. "I wonder if I have one, too!" In their excitement they were forgetting the danger of disturbing others and talking quite loud.

"Yes, mine opens," Gracie went on. "And—oh, yes, I've got candies and something with paper round it and—oh, yes, yes, it is a pin! Not quite like yours, but every bit as pretty!"

"I think they are having a merry Christmas," said the captain, a happy light in his eyes. "And, my love, I wish you the same."

Violet returned the wish, but the children were talking again so they kept quiet to listen.

"Oh, this sweet potato opens, too," Lulu was saying. "And there's something that feels like a stick. Oh, Gracie, Gracie, look! It's a gold pencil, a lovely little gold pencil! Have you one?"

"No, but you haven't a doll."

"Well, I think Santa Claus has been very generous and kind to us."

"Just as good and kind as if he was our own papa," Gracie said with a sweet, silvery laugh.

"The dear, grateful darlings!" exclaimed the captain, his tone half-tremulous with feeling. "I sometimes fear I am almost too indulgent, but it is such a dear delight to give them pleasure."

"And I don't believe it does them the least harm, so long as you do not indulge them in any wrong doing," said Violet. "Love never hurts anybody."

"Merry Christmas, my darlings," he called to them. "Did Santa Claus fill your stockings?"

"Oh, merry, merry Christmas, papa!" they answered. "Yes, sir, Santa Claus or somebody did, and gave us lovely things. We're so very much obliged to him."

As they spoke the door into their little sitting room opened, and Max put in his head, crying in his turn, "Merry Christmas to you all—papa and Mamma Vi, Lulu, and Gracie."

A chorus of merry Christmases answered him. Then Lulu asked, "What did Santa Claus put in your stocking, Maxie?"

"A good deal—about as much as could be crammed into it. There were some very handsome neckties, candies, nuts, and a gold pencil."

"Very nice," commented Lulu. She and Gracie, both talking at once, gave a gleeful account of their discoveries in searching their stockings.

They had hardly finished their narrative when a glad shout from the nursery interrupted them.

"There! Little Elsie has found her stocking, I do believe," said Lulu, starting up to a sitting posture that she might look through the open door into the next room. As she did so a tiny toddling figure clothed in a white night dress and with a well-filled stocking in her arms emerged from the nursery door and ran across the room to the bedside, crying gleefully, "See, mamma, papa, Elsie got."

"What have you got, dear?" asked her father, picking her up and setting her in the bed. "There, pull out the things and let papa and mamma see what they are."

"Mayn't we come and see, too?" asked the three other children.

"Yes," he said. "You can come and peep in at the door but first put on your warm slippers and dressing gowns, that you may not take cold."

Baby Elsie was a merry, demonstrative little thing, and it was great fun for them all to watch her and hear her shouts of delight as she came upon one treasure after another—tiny, brightly dressed dolls and other toys suited to her years.

It did not take her very long to empty the little stocking, and then the captain said to the elder ones, "Now you may close the door, my dears, and get yourselves dressed and ready for the duties and pleasures of the day. I shall be in presently for our usual chat before breakfast."

They made haste with their dressing and were quite ready for their father when he came in some half hour later. They were very lighthearted and merry and full of gratitude for all they had received.

"Dear papa, you are so good to us," they said, twining their arms about his neck as they sat one upon each knee.

"I want to be," he said, caressing them in turn. "I have no greater pleasure than I find in making my children happy. And your grateful appreciation of my efforts makes me very happy."

"But, papa, I—" began Lulu, but then paused.

"Well, daughter, don't be afraid to let me know the thought in your mind," he said kindly.

"I was just wondering why it's right for me to have so many other things and would be wrong for me to have that ring I wanted so badly. But, please, papa," she added quickly and with a vivid blush, "don't think I mean to be naughty about it or want you to spend any more money on me."

"No, dear child, I could not think so ill of you. I did not think it right or wise to buy you the ring, because it would have been spending a great deal for something quite useless and very unsuitable for my little girl. The things I have given you, I considered it right to buy because they will all be useful to you in one way or another."

"The games and storybooks, papa?" asked Gracie with a look of surprise.

"Yes, daughter, people—and especially little folks like Max and Lulu and you—need amusement as a change and rest from work. We can do all the more work in the end if we take time for needed rest and recreation."

"So it won't be time wasted to have our Christmas holidays?" inquired Lulu.

"No, I think not," her father answered.

"Shall we take our new games to Ion with us, papa?" she asked.

"If you wish. I presume Grandma Elsie will not object to your taking any of your possessions with you that you think will be useful or enjoyable to yourselves or others."

"I'm just sure she won't, 'cause she's so kind," said Gracie. "But I s'pose it won't do to take our live new pets?"

"No, but you may safely leave them in Christine's good care."

Breakfast and family worship were over, such of their effects as they would be likely to need during the few days of their expected stay at Ion had been packed and sent, the family carriage was at the door, and everybody nearly ready to get into it, when there was an arrival.

Harold and Herbert had come over on horseback, Rosie and Evelyn in the Ion carriage.

They came running in with their "Merry Christmases and Happy New Years," to receive a return in kind.

"Don't think for a moment that we have come to prevent you from accepting your invitation to Ion as promptly as possible," said Herbert merrily.

"We've come after you and are glad to perceive in your attire signs of readiness to depart."

"But we want to peep at your tree first," put in Rosie. "That's one thing that brought us."

"And we've a proposal to make," said Harold. "Namely, that you all accompany us to the Oaks for a short call on Uncle Horace and the rest—and their Christmas tree, of course—before going over to Ion. The air is delightfully bracing, the roads are good, and if we find there is time, perhaps we might as well extend our ride to the Laurels and give Aunt Rose a call in case we reach them before the family has left home for Ion. What do you say, captain? And you, Vi?"

Both approved, and the children were much pleased with the idea. But they all wanted first to have some time to show their presents to Rosie and Evelyn.

That was granted, and the callers were all taken in to see the tree. Dog, bird, and pussy were exhibited—the pretty things found in the stockings, also. And when all had been duly admired they set out upon their jaunt.

The four little girls—Rosie, Evelyn, Lulu, and Gracie—had the Ion carriage to themselves, and full of life and spirit, enjoyed their drive extremely.

Both calls were made, only a short time spent at each place—hardly more than enough for an exchange of greetings and a hasty examination of the Christmas trees and gifts—then they all drove on to Ion, and the holidays festivities, so long looked forward to by the young people with such eager expectation and delight, began.

The first thing of course was to take a view of the Christmas tree and the presents.

Rosie and Evelyn had declined to tell what they were until they could show them, even refusing to answer Lulu's eager query put while they were driving to the Oaks, "Oh, Rosie, did your mamma give you the set of pearls you wanted so badly?"

"Wait till we get to Ion, and I'll show you all my presents. I received a good many and ought not to fret if I did not get everything I wanted," was what Rosie said in reply, and Lulu, understanding it to mean that there was some disappointment, concluded that the pearls had not been given.

She was more convinced of it when the presents on and about the tree had been displayed and no pearls among them.

Rosie seemed in excellent spirits, however, and Lulu thought she had good reason to be, for the gifts she had showed as hers were both many and desirable.

The guests, all relatives or connections, arrived within a few minutes of each other and for a little while were all gathered together in the tree room— as the children called it for the time—and a very merry, lively set they were.

But presently they scattered to their respective rooms to dress for dinner, or at least to remove their outside garments.

The Raymonds were given the same apartments that had been appropriated to them when living at Ion—Gracie sharing Lulu's room, which communicated directly with the one where the captain and Violet would sleep.

Rosie went with the little girls to their room, to see that they had everything to make them comfortable, because, as she said, they were her guests this time.

"You don't need to change your dresses, I am sure," she remarked as they threw off their coats.

"No," replied Lulu. "These are what papa told us to wear for the rest of the day, and they are as suitable and pretty as any we have."

"Yes, they're lovely," said Rosie. "Your papa does dress you beautifully. I, too, am dressed for the day, and I'd like you both to come to my room for a while. Eva is there taking off her things. She's to share my room while the house is so full. I thought you would want to be Eva's bedfellow, but mamma said your father would want his two little girls close beside him."

"Yes, and that's where we like to be," Lulu answered quickly and in a very pleasant tone. "It seems like home here in this room, too. Now we're ready to go with you, Rosie. We've got our things off and seen that our hair is all right."

Rosie led the way to her room where they found, not only Eva only, but all the little girl cousins, having a chat while waiting for the summons to dinner.

Rosie hastily threw off her coat and hat, then opening a bureau drawer, took from it a jewel case saying with a look of exultation, "I have something to show you, girls—mamma's gift to me." And raising the lid, she displayed a beautiful pearl necklace and bracelets.

"So, she did give them to you!" they exclaimed in surprised chorus, for they had supposed all the presents had been already shown them. "Oh, Rosie, how lovely!"

"I'm ever so glad for you, Rosie," said Lulu. "But I'd about made up my mind that Grandma Elsie thought about buying the pearls for you as papa did about the ring I wanted."

"Mamma didn't buy them," explained Rosie. "They are a set grandpa gave her when she was a little girl. I think they are as handsome as any she could have found anywhere. She said she valued them very highly as his gift, but she could never wear them again. And as I am her own little girl, she was willing to give them to me."

"I think you're pretty big, Rosie," remarked Gracie.

"Yes, in my fifteenth year — almost a woman, as grandpa tells me sometimes — when he wants to make me ashamed of not being wiser and better, I suppose," returned Rosie with a laugh, closing the jewel case and returning it to the drawer. Just then, Betty, the little maid, showed her black face and wooly head at the half-open door with the announcement, "Dinner ready, Miss Rosie, an' all de folks gwine into de dinin' room."

"Very well. We're not sorry to hear it, are we, girls? Let us pair off and go down at once to secure our fair share," said Rosie merrily. "There's just as even number of us — Maud and Lora, Lulu and Eva, Gracie and Rose Lacey, Sydney and I. We're to have a table to ourselves. I asked mamma if we might, and she gave consent."

"I like that," remarked Sydney with satisfaction. "We can have our own fun and eat what we please without anybody to trouble us with suggestions that perhaps such and such article of food may not agree with us."

"But we'll be in the same room with the older folks, and they can overlook us if desired," said Rosie.

"And I'd rather have papa to tell me what to eat," said Gracie.

They were hurrying down the stairs as they talked and reached the dining room just in time to take their places before the blessing was asked by Mr. Dinsmore at the larger table.

It was a grand dinner of many courses, and a good deal of time, enlivened by cheerful chat, was spent at the table.

Quiet games—mirth provoking, yet requiring little exertion of mind or body—filled up the remainder of the afternoon.

After tea they had romping games, but at nine o'clock were called together for family worship. Then, the younger ones, including Lulu and Gracie, went to their beds, very willingly, too, for the day— begun so early because of their eagerness to examine their stockings—had been an unusually long and exciting one. They felt ready for rest.

Gracie indeed was so weary that her father carried her up to her room and did not leave her till she was snug in bed.

She dropped asleep the instant her head touched the pillow, and he stood for a moment gazing a little anxiously at her pale face.

"You don't think Gracie's sick, papa, do you?" asked Lulu softly.

"No, I trust she will be all right in the morning— the darling! But she seems quite worn out now," he sighed softly.

Then, sitting down, he drew Lulu into his arms. "Has it been a happy day with you, dear child?" he asked quietly.

"Yes, papa, very—just full of pleasure. And now that night has come, I'm so glad that I have my own dear papa to hug me close, and that he's going to sleep in the next room to Gracie and me."

"I'm glad, too," he said. "Yes, we have a great deal to be thankful for—you and I. Most of all for

God's unspeakable gift—the dear Saviour whose birth and life and death have bought all our other blessings for us.

"My child, try to keep in mind always, even when engaged in your sports, that you are His and must so act and speak as to bring no disgrace upon His cause. Make it your constant endeavor to honor Him in all your words and ways."

"I do mean to, papa, but, oh, it is easy to forget!"

"I know it, my darling. I find it so, too. But we must watch and pray, asking God earnestly night and morning, on our knees, to keep us from temptation and from sin. We must often send up a swift, silent petition from our hearts at other times when we feel that we need help to overcome.

"I want you, my little daughter, to be particularly on the watch against your besetting sin—an inclination to sudden outbursts of passion. It is not to be expected that everything will move on as smoothly, with so many children and young people together, every day, as they have today. I fear you will be strongly tempted at times to give way to your naturally quick temper."

"Oh, I'm afraid so, too, papa. It would be perfectly dreadful if I should!" she said with a shudder, twining her arm round his neck and hiding her face on his shoulder. "Oh, won't you ask God to help me to keep from it?"

"Yes, I shall. I do every night and morning, and we will ask Him together now."

CHAPTER SEVENTH

IT HAD BEEN GROWING colder all the afternoon and continued to do so rapidly through the night. The next morning at the breakfast table some of the lads announced with great glee that the lakelet was frozen over—the ice so thick and solid that it was perfectly safe for skating in every part.

The news caused quite a flurry of pleasurable excitement among the younger ones of the company.

"I move that we spend the morning there skating," said Zoe.

"How many of us have skates, I wonder?"

"You have, I think. Have you not?" said Edward.

"Yes, yours and mine are in good order. I examined them only the other day."

The captain asked how many knew how to use skates, and from the replies it seemed that all the lads had been more or less accustomed to their use, some of the girls also. Zoe had had quite a good deal of practice before her marriage, a little since.

The winters were usually too mild in this part of the country to give much opportunity for that kind of exercise. She was therefore the more eager to avail herself of this one, for she was very fond of the sport.

Edward, Harold, and Herbert were all in the mood to join her in it and were prepared to do so. Rosie and Max too were equally fortunate, but most of the others had come without skates.

But that difficulty could be easily remedied. Their houses were not far off, nor was the village with its stores where such things could be bought. It was decided to dispatch messengers for the needed supplies.

"Papa," asked Lulu, "may they get a pair for me? I'd like to learn to skate."

He turned to her with an indulgent smile. "Would you? Then you shall. I will send for the skates and give you a lesson in the art myself. I used to be reckoned a good skater in my boyhood. Would my little Gracie like to learn, too?"

"No, thank you, papa. I'd rather walk on the ground or ride."

"You shall ride on the ice if you will, little girlie," said Harold. "I think I can find a conveyance that will suit your taste."

"You're kind to think of it, Uncle Harold," she said with a dubious look. "But I'm so afraid the horses would slip and fall on the ice."

"I think not," he said. "But if they should they will only have to pick themselves up again and go on."

"But I'm afraid they might get hurt and maybe tip me over, too."

Harold only smiled at Gracie as he rose and left the room to immediately attend to the dispatching of the messengers.

Gracie wondered what he meant, but as the older people all about her were busily talking among themselves, she went on quietly with her breakfast and said no more.

"Are you a skater, my dear?" asked the captain, addressing his wife.

"I used to be a tolerably expert one, and I am moderately fond of the exercise," she replied.

"I should like the pleasure of taking you out this morning for a trial of your skill," he said. "Shall I send for skates for you?"

"Thank you, no. I think I have a pair somewhere about the house, and perhaps I can find another set for you."

"There are several pairs of gentlemen's skates," said her mother. "I will have them brought out for the captain to try."

He thanked her, adding that in case a pair should be found to fit, he could have the pleasure of taking his wife out without waiting for the return of the servant dispatched to the village.

Upon leaving the breakfast table they all repaired to the parlor for family worship, as was the custom morning and evening. Then those who had skates and some who wanted the walk and a near view of the skating—Lulu among them—got themselves ready and went to the lakelet, while the others waited for the return of the messenger. Most of them meanwhile gathered about the windows overlooking the lakelet to watch the skaters—Edward, Zoe, Harold, Herbert, Rosie, Evelyn, and Max presently joined by Captain Raymond and Violet, as a pair of skates having been found to fit each of them.

When all were fairly started the scene became very animated and pretty. The two married couples skated well, but Harold, and especially Herbert, far exceeded them. The swift, easy movements with which they glided over the glassy surface of the lake, the exact balancing of their bodies, and the graceful curves they executed called forth many an admiring and delighted exclamation from the onlookers both near at hand and those farther away at the windows of the mansion.

Among the latter were Grandma Elsie, her father, Grandma Rose, and Cousin Ronald.

"Bravo!" cried the two old gentlemen simultaneously as Herbert performed a feat in which he seemed to fairly outdo himself. Mr. Lilburn added, "I feel the old ardor for the sport stir within me at the sight o' the lad's adroit movements. At his age I might have ventured to compete with as expert a skater as he. What say you, Cousin Horace, to a match atween the two auld chaps o' us down there at the lake, noo?"

"Agreed," Mr. Dinsmore said with a laugh. "There are skates that will answer our purpose, I think, and we will set off at once if you'd like."

At that moment Lulu came running in. "The skates have come, Grandma Elsie," she said. "Just as I have gotten back to the house. Papa sent me in because it was too cold, he said, for me to be standing still out there. He'll come for me when Mamma Vi is tired and wants to come in."

"Does she seem to be enjoying it?" asked the person to whom the comments were addressed.

"Oh, yes, ma'am, very much indeed! Aren't you going to try it, too?"

"Yes, do, Elsie," said her father. "And you, too, Rose," to his wife. "Let us all try the sport while we have the opportunity."

The ladies were nothing loath; everybody seemed to catch the spirit of the hour. The skates were quickly distributed and all hurried away to the lake but Lulu and Gracie, who were to stay within doors, by their father's orders, till he came or sent for them.

Lulu, having taken off her hood and coat, now sat before the fire warming her feet. Gracie was watching the skaters from an easy chair by the window.

"It does look like good fun," she said. "Is it very cold out there, Lu?"

"Not so very. The wind doesn't blow, but when you're standing still a while your feet feel right cold. I hardly thought about it though. I was so taken up with watching the skating till papa called to me that it was too cold for me to stand there, and I must come in."

"Papa's always taking care of his children," remarked Gracie.

"Yes," assented Lulu. "He never seems to forget us at all. I 'most wish he would sometimes," she added laughing. "Just once in a while when I feel like having my own way, you know."

"Wasn't he good to send for these for me?" she went on, holding up her new skates and regarding them with much satisfaction. "They're nice ones, and it'll be nice to have him teach me how to use them. I've heard of people getting hard falls learning how to skate, but I think I'll be pretty safe not to fall with papa to attend to me."

"I should think so," said Gracie. "Oh, papa and mamma have stopped, and I do believe they're taking off their skates! At least papa's taking hers off for her, I think."

"Then they're coming in, and we'll get our turn!"

"I don't want to try it."

"No, but you can walk down there, and then you're to have a ride on the ice. You know, Uncle Harold said so."

"I don't know what he meant. And I don't know whether I want to try it, either. Yes, papa and mamma are both coming back."

Violet had soon tired of the sport, and she feared her baby was wanting her. She went on up to the nursery while the captain entered the parlor where his little girls were waiting for his coming.

"Waiting patiently, my darlings?" he said with an affectionate smile. "I know it is rather hard sometimes for little folks to wait. But you may bundle up now, and I will take you out to enjoy the sport with the rest. It will be a nice walk for you, Gracie, and when you get there you will have a pleasant time, I think."

"How, papa?"

"My little girl will see when she gets there," he said. "Ah, here is Agnes with your hood and coat. Now, while she puts them on you, I will see if Lulu's skates are quite right."

They proved to be a good fit, and in a few minutes the captain was on his way to the lakelet with a little girl clinging to each hand.

A pretty boat house stood at the water's edge — on the other side, under the trees — and now close beside it, on the ice, the children spied a small, light sleigh well-supplied with robes of both wolf and bear skins.

"There, Gracie, how would you like to ride in that?" asked her father.

"It looks nice, but — how can it go?" she asked dubiously. "I don't see any horses, papa."

"No, but you will find that it can move without."

Harold had seen them approaching and now came gliding very rapidly toward them on his skates.

"Ah, Gracie, are you ready for your ride?" he asked. "Rosie Lacey and one or two of the other little ones are going to share it with you. Captain, will you lift her in while I summon them?"

"Here we are, Cousin Harold," called a childish voice, and Rose Lacey came running up almost out of breath with haste and excitement, two other little girl cousins following at her heels. "Here we are. Can you take us now?"

"Yes," he said. "I was just about to call you."

In another moment the four were in the sleigh with the robes well tucked around them. Then, Harold, taking hold of the back of the vehicle, gave it a vigorous shove away from the shore. Keeping a tight grip on it, he propelled it quite rapidly around the lake.

It required a good deal of exertion, but Herbert and others came to his assistance. The sleigh made the circuit many times, with its young occupants laughing, chatting, and singing right merrily—the merriest of the merry.

Meanwhile the others enjoyed the skating, perhaps quite as much. The older ladies and the two gentlemen seemed to have renewed their youth and kept up the sport a good deal longer than they had intended in the beginning, while the younger ones, especially the children, were full of mirth and jollity, challenging each other to trials of speed and skill, laughing good-naturedly at little mishaps and exchanging jests and good-humored banter.

Cousin Ronald added to the fun by causing them to hear again and again sounds of jingling sleigh bells and prancing horses in their rear. So distinct and natural were the sounds that they could not help springing aside out of the track of the supposed steeds, turning their heads to see how near they were.

Then shouts of laughter would follow from old and young mingled with shrieks half of fright and half of amusement from the girls.

While all this was going on, Captain Raymond was giving Lulu her first lesson in the use of skates, holding her hand in his and guarding her carefully from the danger of falling.

But for that, she would have fallen several times, for it seemed almost impossible to keep her balance. However, she gained skill and confidence, and at length she asked to be allowed to try it for a little while unaided.

He permitted her to do so but kept very near to catch her in case she should slip or stagger.

She succeeded very well, and after a time he ceased to watch her constantly, remaining near her but taking his eyes off her now and then to see what others were doing. He noted with fatherly pride how Max was emulating the older skaters, and he returned a joyous look and smile given him by Gracie as she swept past in the sleigh.

It presently stopped a few paces away, and he made a movement as if to go and lift her out. But at the sound of a thud on the ice behind him, he turned quickly again to find Lulu down.

She had thrown out her hands in falling, and he felt the thrill of horror as he perceived that one of them lay directly in the path of a skater. Chester Dinsmore was moving with such velocity that he would not be able to check his speed in time to avoid running over her.

But even while he perceived her peril the captain had, with an almost lightening-like movement, stooped over his child and dragged her backward. He was barely in time. Chester's skate just grazed her fingers, cutting off the tip of her mitten. There were drops of blood on the ice, and for a moment her father thought her fingers were off.

"Oh, my child!" he groaned, holding her close in his arms and taking the bleeding hand tenderly in his.

"I'm not hurt, papa. At least, only a little," she hastened to say, while the others crowded about them with agitated, anxious questioning. "Is Lulu hurt?" Did Chess run over her?" "Did the fall hurt her?"

"My fingers are bleeding a little, but they don't hurt much," she answered. "I think his skate went over my mitten, and I suppose my fingers would have been cut off if papa hadn't jerked me back out of the way.

Chester had just joined the group. "I can never be sufficiently thankful for the escape," he said with a slight tremble in his tones. "I could never have forgiven myself if I had maimed that pretty hand, though it was utterly impossible for me to stop myself in time at the headlong rate of speed with which I was moving."

"Your thankfulness can hardly equal her father's," the captain said with emotion almost too big for utterance, as he gently drew off the mitten and bound up the wounded fingers with his handkerchief. "That will do till I get you to the house. Shall I carry you, daughter?"

"Oh, no, papa, I'm quite able to walk," she answered in a cheerful tone. "Please, don't be so troubled. I'm sure I'm not much hurt."

"Allow me to take off your skates for you," Chester said, kneeling down on the ice at their feet and beginning to undo the straps as he spoke. "And I will gladly carry you up to the house, too, if you and your father are willing."

"Oh, thank you, sir, but I'd really rather walk with papa to help me along."

The accident had sobered the party a good deal, and most of them—including the older people and

Lulu's mates—went back to the house with her and her father.

Violet was quite startled and alarmed to see the child brought in with her hand bound up. But when the blood had been washed away, the wounds were found to be little more than skin deep. The bleeding soon ceased and some court plaster was all that was needed to cover up the cuts.

There were plenty of offers of assistance, but the captain chose to do for her himself all that was required to ease her discomfort.

"There, my dear child. You have had a very narrow escape," he said when he had finished, drawing her into his arms and caressing her with great tenderness. "What a heartbreaking thing it would have been for us both had this little hand," taking it tenderly in his, "been robbed of its fingers—far worse to me than to have lost my own."

"And you have saved them for me, you dear father," she said, clinging about his neck and laying her cheek to his. Her eyes were full of tears, a slight tremble in her voice. "But they are yours, because I am," she added, laughing a little hysterically. "Oh, I'm every bit yours—from the crown of my head to the soles of my feet."

"Yes, you are—one of my choice treasures, my darling," he said with emotion. "And my heart is full of great thankfulness to God, our heavenly Father, for enabling me to save you from being so sadly maimed."

"And I do think your Mamma Vi is almost as thankful as either of you," Violet said, coming to his side and softly smoothing Lulu's hair.

They were in the dressing room, no one else present but Gracie and Max.

"I must say, I'm pretty thankful myself," observed the latter jocosely but with a telltale moisture about the eyes. "I shouldn't like to have a sister with a fingerless hand."

"Oh, don't, Max! Don't talk so!" sobbed Gracie. "I just can't bear to think of such dreadful things!"

Her father turned toward her and held out his hand. She sprang to his side, and he put his arm about her.

"The danger is happily past, my dear," he said, touching his lips to her cheek. "Dry your eyes and think of something else, something more pleasant."

"You've had enough of skating, I suppose, Lu? Won't want to try it again, will you?" asked Max.

"Yes, if papa will let me. I'd like to go back this afternoon. But I'd want to keep fast hold of him so that I'd be in no danger of falling," she added, looking lovingly into his eyes.

"I'll not let you try it in any other way for some time to come," he said, stroking her hair. "You must become a good deal more proficient in the use of skates before I can again trust you to go alone, especially where there are so many other and more skillful skaters."

"I don't care for that, papa, but will you take me again this afternoon?"

"We'll see about it when the time comes," he said, smiling at her eager tone and not ill-pleased at this proof of a persevering disposition.

"Oh!" cried Max, glancing toward the window. "It's snowing fast! Dear, it will spoil the skating for all of us!"

"But a good fall of snow will provide other cold weather pleasures, my son," remarked the captain in a cheery tone.

"Yes, sir, so it will," returned Max, echoing the tone.

"And besides, plenty of indoor amusements have been provided," said Violet. "I think we can enjoy ourselves vastly, let the weather outside be what it will."

"I am sure of it," said her husband. "Gracie, did you enjoy your ride?"

"Oh, it was just lovely, papa!" answered the little girl. "The sleigh skimmed along so nicely without a bit of jolting. And then, too, it was such fun to watch the skaters."

A tap at the door, and Rosie's voice was asking, "How is Lulu? Mamma sent me to inquire."

"Come in, Rosie," said the captain. "Mother is very kind, and I am glad to be able to report to her that Lulu is only very slightly hurt — so slightly that doubtless she will be ready to join her mates in any sport that may be going on this afternoon."

Rosie drew near with a look of commiseration on her face but exclaimed in surprise, "Why, your hand isn't even bound up!"

"No, I have just a patch of court plaster on each of three finger tips," returned Lulu, laughingly displaying them.

"But, oh, what a narrow escape!" cried Rosie half breathlessly. "It fairly frightens me to think of it!"

"They'd have all been cut off if it hadn't been for papa," Lulu said with a shudder, hiding her face on his shoulder.

"Oh, Lu, I'm so glad they weren't!" said Rosie. "Eva has been crying fit to break her heart because she was sure that at least the tips of your fingers had been taken off. In fact, I couldn't help crying myself," she added, turning away to wipe her eyes.

"How good of you both!" exclaimed Lulu, lifting her head and showing flushed cheeks and shining eyes. "Papa, sha'n't I go and find Eva and comfort her by letting her see how little I am hurt, after all?"

"Yes, do, my child," he said, releasing her.

The two little girls went from the room together, each with her arm about the other's waist.

"Eva's in my room taking her cry out by herself," said Rosie. "I'd like to go there with you, but I must carry your father's answer to mamma first. Then I'll join you."

The door of Rosie's room stood open. Evelyn sat with her back toward it and Lulu, entering softly, had an arm round her friend's neck before she was aware of her presence.

"Oh, Lu!" cried Evelyn with a start. "Are you much hurt?"

"No, you poor dear. You've been breaking your heart about almost nothing. I hurt my knees a little in falling, and Chester's skate took a tiny slice out of my middle finger and scratched the one each side of it, but that's all. See, they don't even need to be wrapped up."

"Oh, I'm so glad!" exclaimed Eva with a sigh of relief through her tears. Then with a shudder and hugging Lulu close she said, "It would have been too horrible if they'd been cut off! I think skating is dangerous, and I'm not sorry the snow has come to spoil it—for us girls, I mean. The older folks and the boys can take care of themselves, I suppose."

"Oh! I like it!" said Lulu. "I wanted papa to let me go back this afternoon and try it again, and I think he would if the snow hadn't come."

"You surprise me!" exclaimed Evelyn. "If I had come so near losing my fingers, I'd never care to skate any more."

"I always did like boys' sports," remarked Lulu, laughing. "Aunt Beulah used to call me a tomboy, and even Max would sometimes say he believed I was half boy. I was always so glad of a chance to slip off to the woods with him where I could run and jump and climb without anybody by to scold me and tell me I'd tear my clothes. I don't have to do those things without leave now, for papa lets me. He says it's good for my health and that that's of far more importance than my clothes. Oh, we all do have such good times now, at home in our father's house, with him to take care of us!"

"Yes, I'm sure you do, and I'm so glad for you. How happy you all seem! And how brave you are about bearing pain, dear Lu! You are so bright and cheerful, though I'm sure your fingers must ache. Don't they?"

"Yes, some, but I don't mind it very much, and they'll soon be well."

Just then they were joined by several of the other little girls, all anxious to see Lulu and learn whether she was really badly hurt.

They crowded round her with eager questions and many expressions of sympathy first, then of delight in finding her so cheerful and suffering so little.

The next thing was to plan indoor amusements for the afternoon and evening, as evidently the storm had put outdoor pleasures out of the question for that day.

The call to dinner interrupted them in the midst of their talk. It was not an unwelcome summons, for exercise in the bracing winter air had given them keen appetites.

Some of the younger ones who had particularly enjoyed the skating felt a good deal of disappointment that the storm had come to put a stop to it and were, in consequence, quite sober and subdued in their demeanor as they took their seats at the table.

A moment of complete silence followed the asking of the blessing. Then, as Edward took up a carving knife and stuck the fork into a roast duck in front of him, there was a loud, "Quack, quack," that startled everybody for an instant. It was followed by merry peals of laughter from old and young.

A loud squeal came next from a young pig in a dish placed before Mr. Dinsmore, and the song of the blackbird from a pie Grandma Elsie was beginning to serve.

"'Four and twenty blackbirds baked in a pie,'" remarked Mr. Lilburn gravely.

"'When the pie was opened the birds began to sing; wasn't that a dainty dish to set before a king?'"

"Ah ha! Um h'm! Ah ha! History repeats itself. But, Cousin Elsie, I didna expect to be treated to a meal o' livin' creatures in your house."

"Did you not?" she returned with a smile. "Life is full of surprises."

"And grandpa and Ned go on carving without any apparent thought of the cruelty of cutting into living creatures," laughed Zoe.

"And what a singular circumstance that chickens baked in a pie should sing like blackbirds," remarked Grandma Elsie.

"Very, indeed!" said Captain Raymond. "I move that some one prepare an article on the subject for one of the leading magazines."

"No one better qualified for the task than yourself, sir," said his brother-in-law, Mr. Lester Leland.

"You will except our Cousin Ronald," said the captain. "Doubtless he knows more about the phenomenon than any other person present."

"Oh, Cousin Ronald," broke in Walter, "as we can't go skating this afternoon, won't you please tell us young ones some of your famous stories?"

"Perhaps, laddie, but there may be some other amusement provided, and in that case the tales will keep. It strikes me I heard some of the leddies laying plans for the afternoon and evening?" he added, turning inquiringly in Zoe's direction.

"Yes, sir," she said. "We are getting up some tableaux, but we are ready to defer them if anyone wishes to do something else."

"I think we will not tax Cousin Ronald with story telling today," said Grandma Elsie. "He has been making a good deal of exertion in skating, and I know he must feel weary."

"Are you, Cousin Ronald?" asked Walter.

"Well, laddie, I canna deny that there have been times when I've felt a bit brighter and more in the mood for spinning out a yarn, as the sailors say."

"Perhaps you'd like to see the tableaux, too, sir?"

"Yes, I own that I should."

That settled the question. "We will have the tableaux," Grandma Elsie said, and everybody seemed well-satisfied with the decision.

Preparations were begun almost immediately on leaving the table, and pretty much all the short winter afternoon was occupied with them.

They had their exhibition after tea—a very satisfactory one to those who took part and to the spectators alike.

Every child and young person who was desirous to have it so was brought in to one or more of the pictures. Lulu, to her great delight, appeared in several and did herself credit.

"How are the fingers, dear child? Have they been giving you much pain?" the captain asked when he came to her room for the usual goodnight talk, sitting down as he spoke, drawing her to a seat upon his knee, and taking the wounded hand tenderly in his.

"Only a twinge once in a while, papa," she said, putting the other arm round his neck and smiling into his eyes. "It's been a very nice day for me in spite of my accident. Everybody has been so good and kind. I think they tried to give me a pleasant part in as many of the tableaux as they could to comfort me, and really after all it was only a little bit of a hurt."

"But narrowly escaped being a very serious one. Ah, my heart is full of thankfulness to God for you, my darling, and for myself, that the injury was no greater. You might have lost your fingers or you hand; you might even have been killed by falling in such a way as to strike your head very hard upon the ice.

"Did anybody ever get killed in that way, papa?" she asked.

"Yes, I read or heard of one or two such cases, and had it happened to you, I could hardly have forgiven myself for letting go your hand."

"I'm sure you might feel that it was all my own fault, papa," she said tightening her clasp of his neck and kissing him with ardent affection. "It was every bit my own fault because I begged you to let me try it alone."

"No, that could not have excused me, because it is a father's duty to take every care of his child, whether she wishes it or not. And it is my settled purpose to do so henceforward," he said, returning her caress with great tenderness.

CHAPTER EIGHTH

THE STORM CONTINUED through the night but had ceased before the guests at Ion were astir. The ground was thickly carpeted with snow, and clouds still obscured the sun, but there was no wind and the cold was not severe.

"Just the day for a snow fight," remarked Frank Dinsmore, as he and the other lads of the company stood grouped together on the veranda shortly after breakfast. "There's plenty of snow, and it's in prime condition for making into balls."

"So it is," said Herbert Travilla. "And I believe I'm boy enough yet to enjoy a scrimmage in it."

"I, too," said Harold. "Let's build a fort, divide ourselves into two armies—one to besiege and the other to defend it."

The proposition was received with great boyish enthusiasm, and the work of erecting the snow fort began at once.

Some of the girls wanted to help, but they were told their part was to look on.

"I can do more than that," said Rosie, and darting into the house, she presently returned with a small flag. "Here, plant this on your ramparts, Harold," she said. "If you are to defend the fort."

"I don't know yet to which party I shall belong—besiegers or besieged—but I'm obliged for the flag and shall plant it as you advise," he said.

The girls amused themselves snowballing each other, occasionally pausing to watch the progress the lads were making. The older people did the same from the veranda or the windows of the mansion.

The boys were active and soon had their fort—not a large one—constructed, and the flag planted and waving in a slight wind that had sprung up.

Lulu, standing on the veranda steps, clapped her hands in delight as it was flung to the breeze and started singing "The Star-Spangled Banner." All the others joined in, singing with a will.

Then the group of lads divided themselves into two equal companies—Harold taking command of the defenders of the little fort, Chester of the attacking party.

"There are not enough of you fellows," called Sydney. "You'd better let us girls help prepare the ammunition. Women have done such things when men were scarce."

"So they have," replied Chester. "I'll accept such assistance from you if you'll promist to stand back out of danger."

"Then we girls will have to divide into two companies," said Rosie. "For the boys in the fort must have the same kind of help the others do. I'll go to their aid."

"No, no," said Harold. "This is going to be too much of a rough and tumble play for girls. I decline with thanks."

"Ungrateful fellow!" she retorted. "I don't mean to be a bit sorry for you if you are defeated."

"I don't intend that you should even have the opportunity my dear, little sister!" replied Harold.

"Oh, Rosie, I know what we can do!" cried Lulu. "Give them some music."

"Good!" said Sydney. "Wait a minute, boys, till we hunt up a drum and a fife. The band will play on the veranda."

She, Rosie, and Lulu hurried into the house to find the suggested articles as she spoke.

"Yes, I'll lend you mine," shouted Walter after them. "They're up in the playroom—two drums, two mouth organs, a fife, and a trumpet."

The boys waited, employing their time in the preparation of snowballs, and presently the girls came rushing back bringing the musical instruments mentioned by Walter and a jews-harp and accordion beside.

These were quickly distributed, and the band struck up—not with one tune but several all at once—"Hail Columbia," "Yankee Doodle," and the "Star Spangled Banner"—having forgotten in their haste to agree upon a tune.

The music, if music it could be called—was greeted with roars of laughter and ceased at once.

"Oh, this will never do!" cried Maud. "We must settle upon some one of the national airs. Shall it be 'Yankee Doodle'?"

"Yes," they all said and began again, with less discord this time but not keeping very good time.

Harold and his party were in the fort, a huge heap of snowballs beside them.

"Now, man your guns, my lads, and be ready to give a vigorous repulse to the approaching foe," he cried.

Chester had drawn up his men in line of battle. Max was among them.

"Wait!" he cried, "I'm going into the fort."

"What? Going to desert in the face of the enemy?" queried Chester.

"Yes, I can't fight against the flag," pointing to it with uplifted hand. "Fire on the stars and stripes? Never! 'The flag of our Union forever!'"

"Oh, is that all? Well, we're not going to fight against it, my boy. It's ours, and we're going to take it from them and carry it in triumph at the head of the column."

"No, sir, it's ours," retorted Harold. "And we stand ready to defend it to the last gasp. Come on. Take it from us if you can! We dare you to do it!"

"Up then and at 'em, boys!" shouted Chester. "Go double quick and charge right over the breastworks!"

The command was instantly obeyed, the works were vigorously assaulted and as vigorously defended, snowballs flying thick and fast in both directions over the wall.

Max leaped over the breastworks and seized the flag. Harold tore it from his hands, threw him over into the snow on the outside, and replanted the flag on the top of the breastwork.

Max picked himself up, ran round to the other side of the fort, and finding Harold and the other large boys among the defenders each engaged in hand to hand scuffle with a besieger, so that only little Walter was left to oppose him, again leaped over the barrier, seized the flag, leaped back and sped away toward the house, waving it in triumph and shouting, "Hurray! Victory is ours!"

"Not so fast, young man!" shouted back Herbert, bounding over the breastworks and giving chase, All the rest of the group followed, some to aid him in recovering the lost standard, the others to help Max keep it out of his reach.

Herbert was agile and fleet of foot, but so was Max. Back and forth, up and down he ran, now dodging his pursuers behind trees and shrubs, now taking a flying leap over some low obstacle, and speeding on, waving the flag above his head and shouting back derisively at those who were trying to catch him.

It was a long and exciting race, but at last he was caught. Herbert overtook him, seized him with one hand, the flag with the other.

Max wrenched himself free, but Herbert's superior strength compelled him to yield the flag after a very desperate struggle to regain his hold upon it.

Then with a wild hue and cry, Chester's party chased Herbert till after doubling and turning several times, he at length regained the fort and restored the flag to its place.

The next instant Harold and the rest of his fine command regained and reoccupied the fort, the attacking party following close at their heels, and the battle with the snowballs recommenced with redoubled fury.

All this was witnessed with intense interest by the spectators at the windows and on the veranda. At the beginning of the chase, the band forgot to play and dropping their instruments employed themselves in encouraging pursuers or pursued with clapping of hands and shouts of exultation over their exploits.

The contest was kept up for a long time, the flag was taken and retaken again and again till the fort was quite demolished by the repeated assaults, and the snow well trodden all about the spot where it had stood.

The lads, too, found themselves ready to enjoy rest within doors after their continued violent exertion.

Some quiet games filled up the remainder of the morning and the afternoon. In the evening they were ready for another romp in which the girls might have a share, so Stage Coach, Blindman's Buff, and similar games were in demand.

They had been merry and entirely harmonious, but at length a slight dispute arose. Captain Raymond, sitting in an adjoining room conversing with the older guests and members of the family, yet not inattentive to what was going on among the young folks, heard Lulu's voice raised to a higher than ordinary key.

He rose, stepped to the communicating door, and called in a low tone, grave but kindly, "Lulu!"

"Sir?" she replied, turning her face in his direction.

"Come here, daughter," he said. "I want you."

She obeyed quite promptly, though evidently a trifle unwillingly.

He took her hand and led her out into the hall and on into a small reception room, bright and cheery with light and fire, but quite deserted.

"What do you want me for, papa?" she asked. "Please, don't keep me long because we were just going to begin a new game."

He took possession of an easy chair, and, drawing her into his arms and touching his lips to her cheek, he asked, "Can you not spare a few minutes to your father when your mates have had you all day?"

"Why, yes, you dear papa!" she exclaimed with a sudden change of tone, putting her arms about his neck and looking up into his face with eyes full of ardent filial affection. "How nice of you to love me well enough to want to leave the company in the parlors to give a little time to loving me!"

"I love you full well enough for that, my darling," he said, repeating his caresses. "But my call to you was because a tone in my little girl's voice told me she needed her father just at that moment."

She looked up inquiringly, but then with sudden comprehension, she said, "Oh! You thought I was in danger of getting into a passion, and I'm afraid I was. Papa, you are my guardian angel, always on the watch to help me in my hard fight with my dreadful temper. Thank you very, very much!"

"You are entirely welcome, daughter," he said, softly smoothing her hair. "It could hardly be a sadder thing to you than to me—should that enemy of yours succeed in overcoming you again. Try, dear child, to be constantly on the watch against it.

"'Watch ye and pray, lest ye enter into temptation,' Jesus said. The moment that you feel the rising anger in your heart, lift up your heart to Him for strength to resist it."

"I do intend to always, papa," she sighed, tightening her clasp of his neck and laying her cheek to his. "But, oh, it is so, so easy to forget!"

"I know it, dear child, but I can only encourage you to continue the fight with your evil nature, looking ever unto Jesus for help. Press forward in the heavenly way, and if you fall, get up again and go on with redoubled energy and determination. You will win the victory at last, for 'in all these things we are more than conquerors through Him that loved us.'

"Now, if you feel that you are safe in doing so, you may go back to your mates."

There was a sweet expression on Lulu's face as she rejoined her mates, and her manner was gentle and subdued.

"So you've come back," remarked Sydney. "What did your papa want with you?"

"Oh, Syd," exclaimed Rosie. "That's quite private, you know!"

"Oh, to be sure! I beg pardon, Lu," said Sydney.

"You are quite excused," returned Lulu pleasantly. "Papa had something to say to me, that was all," and she glanced up at him with such a loving look, as at that instant he entered the room, that no one could suspect the talk between them had been other than most pleasant.

"Well, you have come back just in time. We are going to play the game of Authors," said Herbert, beginning to distribute the cards.

The words had hardly left his lips when a sharp tap at the window made them all jump. Then a woman's voice spoke in piteous accents.

"Oh, let me in, good people! My baby and I are starving to death and freezing in this bitter winter wind."

"Oh, who is it? Who is it?" cried several of the girls, sending frightened glances in the direction from which the voices had come.

"I'll soon see," said Harold, hurrying toward the window of the room where they were playing.

But a gruff voice spoke from the hall. "Don't mind her, sir. She's a gypsy liar and thief. She stole the baby from its mother."

Harold paused and stood uncertainly in the middle of the floor for an instant. Then, turning quickly, he retraced his steps, went to the hall door, and glanced this way and that.

"There is no one here," he said, then burst into a laugh as, turning round once more, he perceived Mr. Lilburn quietly seated near the open door into the adjoining parlor where the older people were. "Cousin Ronald, may I ask what you know of that gypsy and the stolen child?"

"What do I ken about her, laddie?" queried the old gentleman in his turn. "Wad ye insinuate that I associate wi' sic folks as that?"

"Oh, she's quite a harmless creature, I've no doubt," laughed Harold.

"Oh, Uncle Harold, please let her in," pleaded Gracie with tears in her sweet, blue eyes.

"Why, my dear little Gracie, there's nobody there," he answered.

"But how can we be sure if we don't look, Uncle Harold? Her voice sounded so very real."

"What is the matter, Gracie dear?" asked a sweet voice, as a beautiful lady came swiftly from the adjoining parlor and laid her soft, white hand on the little girl's head.

"Oh, Grandma Elsie, we heard a woman begging to come in out of the cold, and—oh, there, don't you hear her?"

"Oh, let me in, dear good ladies and gentlemen! I'm freezing and starving to death!" wailed the voice again.

By this time all the occupants of the other parlor were crowding into this one.

"Captain," asked Grandma Elsie, "will you please step to the window and open it?"

"Mother, Cousin Ronald is responsible for it all," laughed Harold.

"We may as well let Gracie see for herself," Mrs. Travilla replied in a kindly indulgent tone.

Harold at once stepped to the window, drew back the curtains, raised the sash, and threw open the shutters, giving a full view of all the grounds on that side of the house. The clouds had cleared away, and the moon was shining down on snow-laden trees and shrubs and paths and parterres carpeted with the same, but no living creature was to be seen anywhere.

Gracie, holding fast to her father's hand, ventured close to the window and sent searching glances from side to side, but then with a sigh of relief said, "Yes, I do believe it was only Cousin Ronald. I'm ever so glad the woman and her baby are not freezing."

At that everybody laughed, and timid, sensitive little Gracie hid her blushing face on her father's shoulder as he sat down and drew her to his side.

"Never mind, darling," he said soothingly, passing an arm affectionately about her and smoothing her curls with his other hand. "It is good natured amusement. We all know what you meant and love you all the better for your tenderness of heart toward the poor and suffering."

"Yes, dear child, your papa is quite right, and I fear we were not very polite or kind to laugh at your innocent speech," said Grandma Elsie.

At that instant the tap on the window was repeated, then the voice spoke again, but in cheerful tones. "Dinna fret ye bit, bonny lassie. I was but crackin' me jokes. I'm neither cauld nor hungry, and my bairns grew to be men and women lang syne."

"There now! I know it's Cousin Ronald," laughed Rosie. "And indeed I should hope he was neither cold nor hungry here in our house."

"If he is," said Grandma Elsie, giving the dear, old gentleman a pleasant smile, "we will set him in the warmest corner of the ingleside and order him some refreshments."

"I vote that it be carried out immediately," said Edward. "Harold, if you will conduct our kinsman to the aforesaid seat, I will, with mamma's kind permission, ring for the refreshments."

Harold and Herbert stepped promptly forward, each offering an arm to the old gentleman.

"Thank ye, laddies," he said. "But I'm no' so infirm that I canna cross the room wi'out the help o' your strong young arms, and being particularly comfortable in the chair I now occupy, I shall bide here, by your leave."

"Then, if you feel so strong, would it tire you to tell us a story, Cousin Ronald?" asked Walter. "We'd like one ever so much while we're waiting for the refreshments."

"The refreshments are ready and waiting in the dining room. You are all invited to walk out there and partake of them," said Grandma Elsie as the servants drew back the sliding doors, showing a table glittering with china, cut-glass, and silver loaded with fruits, nuts, cakes, confectionery, and ices and adorned with a profusion of flowers from the conservatories and hothouses.

"Don't you wish you were grown up enough to call for whatever you might fancy from that table?" whispered Rosie to Lulu as they followed their elders to its vicinity.

"Yes—no. I'm very willing to take whatever papa chooses to give me," returned Lulu. "You see," she added, laughing at Rosie's look of mingled surprise and incredulity, "there have been several times he has let me have my own way, and I didn't find it at all nice. So now I've really grown willing to be directed and controlled by him."

"That's a very good thing."

"Yes, especially as I'd have to do it anyhow. Papa, may I have something?" she asked, as at that moment he drew near.

"Are you hungry?" he queried in turn.

"Yes, sir."

"Then you may have some ice cream, a little fruit, and a small piece of sponge cake."

"Not any nuts or candies?"

"Not tonight, daughter. Sometime tomorrow you may have some of those things."

"Thank you, sir. That will do nicely," she responded in a cheerful, pleasant tone and with a loving look and smile up into his face.

She felt amply rewarded by the approving, affectionate look he gave her in return.

"I shall help you presently when I have waited upon Evelyn and Rosie," he said. "What will you have, my dears?"

When the refreshments had been disposed of, it was time for the usual short evening service, then for the younger ones to go to their beds.

Captain Raymond stepped out upon the veranda and paced to and fro. Presently Max joined him. "I came to say goodnight, papa" he said.

"Ah, good night, son," returned the captain, pausing in his walk, taking the hand Max held out to him, and clasping it affectionately in his. "You had a fine, exciting game this morning out there on the lawn. I was glad to hear my boy avow his attachment to the glorious old flag his father has sailed under for so many years. I trust he will always be ready to do so when such an avowal is called for, as long as he lives."

"Yes, indeed, sir! It's the most beautiful flag that waves, isn't it?"

"None compare to it in my esteem," his father answered with a pleased laugh.

CHAPTER NINTH

BEFORE MORNING, THE weather had moderated very much, a thaw had set in, and the snow was going rapidly.

"Well, what sports shall we contrive for today?" asked Herbert at the breakfast table. "Certainly both skating and snow fights are entirely out of the question now."

"Entirely!" echoed Harold. "All other outdoor sports also, for a drizzling rain is beginning to fall and the melting snow has covered roads and paths with several inches of water."

"We have some games for the house that you have not tried yet," said their mother. "We have Table Croquet, Parlor Quoits, Jack-straws, and others."

"And I have a new game that papa gave me this Christmas—The Flags of all Nations," remarked Lulu. "I brought it with me."

"We will be glad to see it," said Harold.

"It is probably improving as well as entertaining," remarked Zoe. "I should judge so from the name."

"I think you will find it both," said the captain.

"So you would find Corn and Beans, too, Aunt Zoe," said Max. "Papa gave it to me, and we tried it Christmas Eve at home and found it very funny."

The morning and most of the afternoon were occupied with these games, which seemed to afford much enjoyment to the children and young people.

It was the winding up of their wonderful Christmas festivities at Ion, and all were in the mood for making it as merry and mirthful as possible. Some—the Raymonds among others—would leave shortly after tea, the rest by or before bedtime.

They finished the sports of the afternoon with two charades. The older people were the spectators, the younger ones the actors.

Mendicant was the word chosen for the first.

A number of the boys and girls came trooping into the parlor, each carrying an old garment, a thimble on their finger, and a needle and thread in hand. Seating themselves, they fell to work.

Zoe was patching an old coat, Lulu an apron, Gracie a doll's dress. Eva and Rosie each had a worn stocking drawn over her hand and was busily engaged in darning it. The other girls were mending gloves, the boys old shoes. As they worked they talked among themselves.

"Zoe," said Maud, "I should mend that coat very differently than you are."

"How would you mend it?" asked Zoe.

"With a patch much larger than that you are sewing on it."

"I shouldn't mend it that way," remarked Sydney. "I'd darn it."

"Thank you both for your kind and disinterested advice," sniffed Zoe. "But I learned how to mend before I ever saw you. And I should mend those gloves in a better way than you are taking."

"If you know so well how to mend, Madam Zoe, will you please give me some instruction about mending this shoe?" said Herbert. "Cobbling is not in my line."

"Neither is it in mine, Sir Herbert," she returned, drawing herself up with a lofty air.

"Such silly pride! They should mend their ways if not their garments," remarked Maud in quite a scornful aside.

"One should think it beneath her to mend even a worn stocking," said Rosie.

"No," responded Eva. "She should mend it well."

"Your first syllable is not hard to guess, children," said Mrs. Dinsmore. "Evidently it is mend.

With that the actors withdrew, and presently Chester Dinsmore returned alone, marching in and around the room with head erect and with pompous air. His clothes were of fine material and fashionable cut. He wore handsome jewelry, sported a gold-headed cane, and strutted to and fro gazing about him with an air of lofty disdain as of one who felt himself superior to all upon whom his glances fell.

Harold presently followed him into the room. He was dressed as a country swain, came in with a modest, diffident air, and for a while stood watching Chester curiously from the opposite side of the room. Then, crossing over, he stood before him, hat in hand, and bowed low. "Sir," he said respectfully, "will you be so kind as to tell me if you are somebody particular? I'm from the country, and I shouldn't like to meet any great man and not know it."

"I, sir?" cried Chester, drawing himself up to his full height and swelling with importance. "I? I am the greatest man in America, the greatest man of the age. I am Mr. Smith, sir, the inventor of the most delicious ices and confectionery ever eaten."

"Thank you, sir," returned Howard with another low bow. "I shall always be proud and happy to have met so great a man."

Laughter, clapping of hands, and cries of "I! I!" among the spectators grew, as the two withdrew by way of the hall.

Soon the young actors flocked in again. A book lay on a table, quite near the edge. With a sudden jerk, Herbert threw it on the floor.

Rosie picked it up and replaced it, saying, "Can't you let things alone?"

"Rosie, why can't you let the poor boy alone?" whined her cousin, Lora Howard. "No one has ever known me to be guilty of such an exhibition of temper. It's positively wicked."

"Oh, you're very good, Lora," sniffed Zoe. "I can't pretend to be half so perfect."

"Certainly, I can't," said Eva.

"I can't."

"I can't," echoed Lulu, Max, and several others.

"Come now, children, can't you be quiet a bit?" asked Harold. "I can't auction off these goods unless you are attending to the business and ready with your bids."

Setting down a basket he had brought in with him, he took an article from it and held it high in the air.

"We have here an elegant lace veil worth perhaps a hundred dollars. It is to be sold now to the highest bidder. Somebody give us a bid for this beautiful piece of costly lace, likely to go for a tithe of its real value."

"One dollar," said Rosie.

"One dollar, indeed! We could never afford to let it go at so low a figure. We can't sell this elegant and desirable an article of ladies' attire at so ridiculously low a price."

"Ten dollars," said Maud.

"Ten dollars, ten dollars! This elegant and costly piece of lace going at ten dollars!" cried the auctioneer, holding it higher still and waving it to and fro. "Who bids higher? It is worth ten times that paltry sum. It would be dirt cheap at twenty. Somebody bid twenty. Don't let a chance escape you. You can't expect another such. Who bids? Who bids?"

"Fifteen," bid Zoe.

"Fifteen, fifteen! This lace veil, worth every cent of a hundred dollars, going at fifteen? Who bids higher? Now's your chance. You can't have it much longer. Going, going at fifteen dollars—this elegant veil, worth a cool hundred. Who bids higher? Going, going, gone!"

"Can't," exclaimed several of the audience as the veil was handed to Zoe, and the whole company of players retired.

They shortly returned, all dressed in shabby clothing, some with knapsacks on their backs, some with old baskets on their arms—an unmistakable troop of beggars, passing round among the spectators with whining petitions for cold victuals and pennies.

A low growl instantly followed by a loud, fierce bark startled players and spectators alike and called forth a slight scream from some of the little ones.

"That auld dog o' mine always barks at sic a troop o' mendicants," remarked Cousin Ronald quietly. "I ken *mendicant*'s the word, lads and lasses, and ye hae acted it out wi' commendable ingenuity and success."

"You couldn't have made a better guess if you belonged to the universal Yankee nation, cousin," laughed Herbert.

They retired again, and in a few minutes Eva and Lulu came in dressed in traveling attire, each with a satchel in her hand.

"This must be the place, I think," said Eva, glancing from side to side, "but there seems to be no one in."

"They may be in directly," said Lulu. "Let us sit down and rest in these comfortable-looking chairs while we wait."

They seated themselves, and as they did so Zoe and Maud walked in.

They, too, were dressed as travelers and carried satchels. The four shook hands, Zoe remarking, "So you got in here before us! How did you come?"

"In the stage," answered Lulu.

"Ah! One travels so slowly in that! We came in the cars," said Maud.

"Yes," said Zoe, "in the train that just passed."

"Let us go back in the cars, Lu," said Eva.

"Yes, in the same train they take. Oh! Who is this coming? He acts like a crazy man!" as Frank Dinsmore entered, gesticulating wildly, rolling his eyes, and acting altogether very much like a madman.

Chester was following close at his heels.

"Don't be alarmed, ladies," he said. "He shall not harm you. I'll take care of that. I have my eye on him all the time — never let him out of my sight. I am his keeper."

"But he's dangerous, isn't he?" they asked, shrinking from Frank's approach, as if in great fear.

"Not while I am close at hand," said Chester. "I'll see that he disturbs no one."

"I think it would be well for us to go now, girls," said Zoe. "Let us ask the driver of that stage to take us in. Then we'll be safe from this lunatic."

They hurried out, and in another minute Chester and Frank followed.

Then Edward came in, walked up to the fire, and stood leaning against the mantelpiece in seemingly thoughtful mood. But as the lady travelers again appeared at the door, he started and went forward to receive them.

"Walk in, ladies," he said. "Walk into the parlor. Pray be seated," handing them chairs. "Now what can I do for you?"

"You are the innkeeper?" asked Zoe.

"At your service, madam. Do you wish a room? Or rooms?"

"Yes, we will have two. Let them be adjoining, if possible, sir."

"Certainly, madam. We can accommodate you in that and will be happy to do so."

Then turning to the spectators, "Can you tell us our word, ladies and gentlemen?" he asked.

"Innkeeper," came the prompt response from several voices.

"Quite correct," he said. Then with a sweeping bow, "This closes our entertainment for the evening. With many thanks for their kind attention, we bid our audience a grateful adieu."

Shortly after, tea was served, and upon conclusion of the meal, the guests began to take their departure.

The family separated for the night earlier than usual, but Harold and Herbert followed their mother to her dressing room, asking if she felt too weary for a little chat with them.

"Not at all," she said with her own sweet smile. "I know of nothing that would afford me greater satisfaction than one of the old-time motherly talks with my dear college boys. So, come in, my dears, and let us have at it."

Harold drew forward an easy chair for her, but she declined it. "No, I will sit on the sofa, so that I can have you close to me, one on each side," she said.

"That will suit your boys exactly, mamma, if you will be quite comfortable," said Herbert, placing a hassock for her feet as she seated herself.

"Quite," she returned, giving a hand to each as they placed themselves beside her. "Now remember that your mother will be glad of your confidence in everything that concerns you—great or small. Nothing that interests you or affects your happiness in the very least can fail to have an interest for her."

"We know it, dearest mamma," saiad Harold. "We are most happy in the assurance that such is the fact."

"Yes," assented Herbert, lifting her hand to his lips. "It is that which makes a private chat with our mother so great a delight—that and our mutual love. Mamma, dear, I can not believe I shall ever meet another woman who will seem to me at all comparable to my dearly loved and honored mother."

"Such words from the lips of my son are very sweet to my ear," she responded, a tender light shining in her eyes. "And yet for your own sake I hope you are mistaken. I would have all my children know the happiness to be found in married life where mutual admiration, esteem, and love are so great that the two are as one."

"Such a marriage as yours, mamma?"

"Yes, there could not be a happier. But I am looking far ahead for my college boys," she added with a smile. "At least I trust so, for you are young yet to be looking for life partners."

"I don't think either of us has begun on that thus far, mamma," said Harold. "At present we are more solicitous to decide the important question, what shall our principal life work be? And in that we desire the help of our mother's counsel and to follow her wishes."

"It is a question of very great importance," she said. "For your success and usefulness in life will depend very largely upon your finding the work your heavenly Father intends you to do and for which you are best fitted by the talents He has given you.

"But I thought you had both decided upon the medical profession, and I was well content with your choice, for it is a most noble and useful calling."

"So we thought, mamma, but recently our hearts have been so moved at the thought of the millions perishing for lack of a saving knowledge of Christ. It has become a momentous question with each of us whether he is called to preach the gospel, especially in the mission field—at home or abroad."

Her eyes shone through glad tears. "My dear boys," she said with emotion, "to have sons in the ministry I should esteem the greatest honor that could be put upon me. There can be no higher calling than that of an ambassador for Christ, no greater work than that of winning souls."

"So we both think," said Herbert. "Mamma, you are willing we should go and labor wherever we may be called in the providence of God?"

"Yes, oh, yes! You are more His than mine. I dedicated you to His service even before you were born and many times afterward. I would not dare stand in your way, nor would I wish to. Dearly as I love you both and sweet as your presence is to me, I am more than willing to deny myself the joy of having you near me for the sake of the Master's cause, that you may win the reward of those to whom He will say at last, 'Well done, good and faithful servant; enter thou into the joy of the Lord.' Are you particularly drawn to the foreign field?"

"No, mamma," answered Harold. "The cause is one; 'the field is the world.' But while we are deeply interested in foreign missions and desirous to do all we can to help there, we feel that their prosperity depends upon the success of the work at home and that the cause of home missions is the cause of our country also. For that cause we would labor and give as both patriots and Christians.

"Look at the dangers threatening our dear native land—and the cause of Christ also—from vice and illiteracy, all ever on the increase from paupers, the insane, anarchists, and criminals. Ah, how surely and speedily they will sweep away our liberties, both civil and religious, unless we rouse ourselves and put forth every energy to prevent it! Never a truer saying than that 'eternal vigilance is the price of liberty!' And nothing can secure it to us but the instruction and evangelization of these dangerous classes. Is it not so, mamma?"

"Yes," she assented. "I am satisfied that the gospel of Christ is the only remedy for those threatening evils, the only safeguard of our liberties, and the only true salvation for a lost and ruined world.

"And, my dear boys, if you devote yourselves to that work it shall be your mother's part, your mother's joy, to provide the means for your support. I can not go into the world myself, so the sending of my sons and supporting them while they labor, must be my contribution to the cause.

"But I see no reason why you should give up the idea of studying medicine, since so many medical missionaries are needed. My plan would be to prepare you for both preaching and practicing, if you have talent for both."

"We have thought of that," said Harold. "And as you approve, dearest mamma, we will hope to carry it out."

"I am glad, mamma, that you have large means and the heart to use them in the work of spreading abroad the glad tidings of salvation through Christ," Herbert remarked.

"Yes," she said, "it is both a responsibility and a privilege to be entrusted with so much of my Lord's money. Pray for your mother, my dear boys, that she may have both the grace and the wisdom to dispense it aright."

"We will, mamma. We do. And, oh, how often we rejoice in having a mother to whom we can confidently apply in behalf of a good cause! You have many times given us the joy of relieving misery and providing instruction for the ignorant and depraved."

"It has been a joy to me to be able to do so," she said thoughtfully. "Yet I fear I have not denied myself as I ought for the sake of giving largely."

"Mamma, you have always given largely since I have been old enough to understand anything about such matters," interrupted Harold warmly. "Yes, very largely."

"If everyone had given and would give as largely in proportion to means," remarked Herbert, "the Lord's treasury would be full to overflowing. Is it not so, Harold?"

"Surely, and mamma has never been one to spend unnecessarily on herself," replied Harold, fondly caressing the hand he held.

"It has been my endeavor to be a faithful steward," she sighed. "And yet I might have given more than I have. I have been giving only of my income. I could give some of the principal. And I have a good many valuable jewels that might be turned into money for the Lord's treasury.

"I have thought a good deal about that of late and have talked to my daughters in regard to the matter. I thought it but right to consult them, because the jewels would be a part of their inheritance, and I wish you two to have some say about it also, as fellow heirs with them."

She paused, and both lads answered quickly that they thought the jewels should all go to their sisters.

"No, you and your future wives should have a share also," she replied smilingly. "That is, if I retained them all. And that being understood, are you willing to have most of them disposed of and the proceeds used in aid of home and foreign missions?"

Both gave a hearty assent.

"Thank you, my dears," she said. "And now having already consulted with your grandfather and older brother, winning their consent and approval, I consider the matter settled.

"A few of my jewels, dear to me as mementos of the past, I shall retain. Also, I shall keep a few others that would not sell for nearly what they are really worth to us. But the rest I intend to have sold, and the money used for the spread of the gospel in our own and heathen lands."

"I am convinced you could not make a better investment, mamma," Harold said, his eyes shining with pleasure.

"Yes, you are right," she returned. "It is an investment—one that cannot possibly fail to give a grand return, for does He not say, 'He that hath pity upon the poor lendeth to the Lord; and that which he hath given will He pay him again?'

"Who was it—Dean Swift, if I remember aright—who preached a charity sermon from that text—'If you like security, down with the dust'?"

"And you do like security, mamma. You prefer it to any other, I am quite sure," said Herbert. "But what a fine specimen of a charity sermon that was! Both powerful and brief. Doubtless many of the hearers were greatly relieved that they had not to listen to a long, dull harangue on the subject and seemed all the more disposed to give liberally on that account."

"Yes, do not forget to act upon that idea when your turn comes to preach a sermon on that subject," Harold said, giving his younger brother a mischievous smile.

"And let us not forget the lesson of the text when the appeal comes to us," added their mother. "Oh, my dear boys, what a privilege it is to be permitted to make such investments! And to be sowers of good seed whether by personal effort or in providing the means for sending out others as laborers. Let us endeavor to be of the number of those who sow largely in both ways, for 'He which soweth sparingly shall reap also sparingly, and he that soweth bountifully shall reap also bountifully.'

"And the harvest is sure at the end of the world, if not sooner. And whether we give in one way or the other, let us not do it 'grudgingly or of necessity,' but joyfully and with all our hearts, for God loveth a cheerful giver."

"Mamma," said Harold earnestly, "we do both feel it a great and blessed privilege to be permitted to be co-workers with God for the advancement of his cause and kingdom."

And with that, the conversation turned upon other themes,. Presently the boys kissed their dear mother goodnight and withdrew lest they should rob her of needed rest.

CHAPTER TENTH

"Home again, and it is nice to get home!" exclaimed Lulu, skipping up the steps of the veranda and across into the wide hall where all was light and warmth and beauty.

Violet and Gracie had preceded her, and her father was following with little Elsie in his arms.

"I am glad to hear you say that. I'm so glad my little daughter appreciates her home," he said in a cheery tone.

"I'd be a strange girl, papa, if I didn't appreciate such a home as this is," she returned with warmth, smiling up into his face. "Don't you say so, Max?" catching sight of her brother who, riding his pony, had arrived some minutes ahead of the carriage and was now petting and stroking his dog at the farther end of the hall.

"Yes, indeed!" he answered. "I think if we weren't happy and contented in this home, we oughtn't to have any at all. Papa, Prince is a splendid fellow!" stroking and patting the dog's head as he spoke.

"So I think," said the captain.

"And I, too," said Violet. "He is a very acceptable addition to the family. My dear, home does look exceedingly attractive to me and to the children. But little Elsie's eyes are closing. Mamma must see her babies to bed."

"I wonder where my little pussy is?" Gracie was saying from the library door. "I thought she'd be lying on the rug before the fire here, like she was the other night, but she isn't."

"Oh, and my Polly!" cried Lulu. "Is she in there?"

"I will carry Elsie to the nursery, my love," said the captain. "Lulu and Gracie, you may perhaps find your pets in your own little sitting room."

"Oh, yes!" they cried in chorus and started up the stairs after their father and Violet.

Outside the night was cold, but within the house the atmosphere was that of summer. Doors stood open, and in the halls and the rooms used by the family, lights were burning. Also, the air was sweet and fragrant with a faint odor of roses, heliotrope, and migonette, coming from the conservatory and from vases of cut flowers placed here and there. All this was the result of Captain Raymond's kind forethought for the comfort and pleasure of wife and children and the careful carrying out of his orders by the faithful housekeeper, Christine.

No wonder home looked so attractive to its returning occupants, even coming from a former one quite as beautiful and luxurious.

"Oh, how sweet it does look in here!" exclaimed both the little girls as they entered their own little sitting room.

"Oh! And there is my pussy lying on the rug all curled up like a soft, round ball!" added Gracie. "You are having a nice nap, pretty kitty, and I don't mean to wake you. But I must pet you just a little bit," dropping down beside her and gently stroking the soft fur.

"And there's my Polly in her cage and fast asleep, too, I do believe," said Lulu. "I want ever so much to hear her talk, but I'll be as good to her as you are to your pet, Gracie. I won't wake her.

"Now we must take off our things, Gracie, for you know papa always says that we mustn't keep them on in the house and that we must put them away in their places."

"Yes, but I'm so tired! Papa would let me wait a minute or two."

"Of course, you poor, little, weak thing! I'll take them off for you and put them away, too, and you need hardly move," Lulu said, hastily throwing off her own coat and hat.

"Dear Lu, you're just as good to me as can be!" sighed Gracie in tender, grateful accents. "I really don't know what I'd ever do without my big sister."

"Somebody else would take care of you," said Lulu, flushing with pleasure nevertheless. "There now, I'll go and put both our things in their right places."

When she came back she found Gracie brimming over with delight because the kitten had awakened, crept into her lap, and curled itself up there for another nap.

"Oh, Lu, just see!" she cried. "I do believe she's fond of me. Isn't it nice?"

"Yes, very nice, but you're burning your face before that bright fire. Oh, you do need your big sister to take care of you!" lifting a screen between Gracie and the glowing grate.

Then, seating herself on a hassock, "Now put your head in my lap and stretch yourself out on the rug. You can rest nicely that way, and we'll have a good talk. Such a nice, big, soft rug as this is! I should think it must have taken several big sheep skins to make it, and it was so good of papa to have it put here for us."

"Yes, indeed! Our dear papa! How I do love him! He's always doing kind things for us."

"Yes, Gracie, if I were only good like you and didn't ever do and say naughty things that made him feel sad!" sighed Lulu. "Oh, do you know we are going to have a party on New Year's? All the folk that were at Ion are to come—the grown up ones to papa and Mamma Vi's company, and the young ones yours and Maxie's and mine."

"Yes, I know, and we're all to go to Fairview to spend Monday."

"Won't it be nice?"

"Yes—" came the rather doubtful answer. It was almost a "but I 'most think I like being at home the best of all."

"Why? Didn't you enjoy yourself at Ion?"

"Yes, but I believe I'm a little bit tired now."

"Tired?"

"Yes—of being with so many folks. It's nice for a while, but after that it sort of wears me out. I'm glad to get back to my own dear home where I can be just as quiet as ever I please."

"Oh, there is papa!" exclaimed Lulu, turning her head and seeing him standing in the open doorway.

He was smiling on his darlings, thinking what a pretty picture they made—the little slender figure on the rug with the kitten closely cuddled in her arms, the golden head lying in Lulu's lap, while her blooming face bent tenderly over her sister's, one hand toying with her soft ringlets.

"Tired, Gracie, my dear?" he asked, coming quickly forward and stooping to scan the small, pale face in loving solicitude.

"Only a little, dear papa," she answered with a patient smile up into his face. "I think I shall be quite rested by tomorrow morning, and I'm so glad we're at home again."

"Yes, and just now the best place in it for my weary little girl is her bed. Lulu and I will get you there as soon as we can."

"Mustn't I stay up for prayers?"

"No, darling. You are too tired and sleepy to get any good from the service. I see your eyes can hardly keep themselves open."

"I believe they can't, and I shall be so glad to go right to my nice bed," she returned sleepily, pushing the kitten gently from her.

So she was lifted to her father's knee, and Lulu went for her nightdress.

In a few minutes she was resting peacefully in her bed, while the captain and Lulu went down hand in hand to the library, where they found Max sitting alone, reading.

He closed his book as they entered, rose, and wheeled an easy chair nearer the fire for his father, who took it with a pleasant, "Thank you, my son," and drew Lulu to a seat upon his knee. "What were you reading, Max?" he asked.

"*Story of the United States Navy for Boys*," answered the lad. "Papa, would you be willing for me to go into the navy?"

"If you have a strong inclination for the life, my boy, I shall throw no obstacle in your way."

"Thank you, sir. I sometimes think I should like it, yet I'm not quite sure I'd rather be there than anywhere else."

"You must be quite sure of your inclination before we move in the matter," returned his father.

"Is there something you would rather prefer for me, papa?"

"If I were quite sure you were called of God to the work, I should rather see you a preacher of the gospel, an ambassador for Christ, than anything else. Yet, if you lack the talent, or consecration, you would be better out of the ministry than in it."

"I'm glad I'm not a boy and don't have to go away from home and papa," Lulu said, nestling closer in her father's arms.

"Home's a delightful place and nobody loves to be with papa more than I do," said Max. "But for all that I'm glad I'm going to be a man and able to do a man's work in the world."

"And I," said the captain, "am glad that God has given me both sons and daughters, and that you two are satisfied to be what God has made you."

For some moments no one spoke again. Then Lulu remarked thoughtfully, "This is the last Saturday, and tomorrow will be the last Sunday of the old year. Papa, do you remember the talk we had together a year ago?"

"On the last Sunday of that year? Yes, daughter, quite well. And now it is time for another retrospect and fresh resolutions to try to live better by the help of Him who is the Strength of His people, their Shield and Helper."

"It hasn't been nearly so good a year with me as I hoped it would be," sighed Lulu.

"Yet an improvement upon the one before it, I think," remarked her father in tones of encouragement. "You have not, so far as I know, indulged, even once, in a fit of violent anger. Knowing my little girl as most truthful and very open with me, I certainly believe that if she had been in a passion, she would have come to me with an honest confession of her fault."

"I'm sure Lu would," said Max. "And I do think she has improved very much."

"No, I haven't been in a passion, papa, and I hope if I had, I wouldn't have been deceitful enough to try to hide it from you. But, oh, I've been very, very naughty two or three times in other ways, you know. And you were so good to forgive me and keep on loving me in spite of it all."

"Dear child!" was all he said in reply, accompanying the words with a tender caress.

"I, too, have come a good deal short of my resolves," observed Max with a regretful sigh. "Yet, I suppose we have both done better than we should if we hadn't made good resolutions."

"No doubt of it," said his father. "I feel it to be so in my case, though I, too, have fallen far short of the standard I set for myself. But, shall we not try again, my children?"

"Oh, yes, sir, yes!"

"And try not only to make the new year better—if we are spared to see it—but also the three remaining days of the old?"

"Yes," sighed Lulu, "perhaps I may get into a dreadful passion yet before the year is out."

"I hope not, daughter," her father said. "But watch and pray, for only so can you be safe. There is One who is able to keep you from falling. Cling close to Him like the limpet to the rock."

"Oh, I will!" she replied in an earnest tone. "But papa, what is a limpet? I don't remember ever having heard of it before."

"It is a shellfish of which there are numerous species exhibiting a great variety of both form and color. The common limpet is most abundant on the rocky coasts of Britain. They live on the rocks between low and high tide marks.

"They move about when the water covers them, but when the tide is out, remain firmly fixed to one spot—so firmly, that unless surprised by a sudden seizure, it is almost impossible to drag or tear them from the rock without breaking the shell."

"How can they hold so tight?" asked Max.

"The animal has a round or oval muscular foot by which it clings, and its ability to do so is increased by a viscous or sticky secretion."

"Please, tell us some more about them, papa," requested Lulu, looking greatly interested. "Have they mouths? And do you know what they eat?"

"Yes, they have mouths, and they live upon seaweed, eating it by means of a long, ribbon-like tongue covered with rows of hard teeth. The common limpet—which, as I told you, lives on the British coast—has no fewer than one hundred and sixty rows, twelve teeth in a row. How many does that make, Max?"

"Nineteen hundred and twenty," answered the lad after a moment's thought.

"Right," said his father. "The tongue when not in use lies folded deep in the interior of the limpet."

"Are their shells pretty, papa?" Lulu asked.

"Those of some of the limpets of warmer climates are very beautiful," he answered. "Large, too. I have seen them on the western coast of South America a foot wide—so large that they are often used as washbasins."

"Oh, I'd like to have one!" she exclaimed. "Is it for their shells people try to pull them off the rocks?"

"It may be so in some instances, but the limpet is used for food and also as bait by the fisherman.

"Try, my children, to remember what I have been telling you about it, but most of all let your thoughts dwell upon the lesson to be drawn from its close clinging to the rock.

"God is often spoken of in the Scriptures as His people's rock, because He is their strength, their refuge, their asylum, as the rocks were in those places whither the children of Israel retired in case of an unexpected attack from their foes.

"David says, 'The Lord is my rock and my fortress . . . Who is a rock save our God?'

"Jesus is the rock on which we must build our hope of salvation. Any other foundation will be as the sand upon which the foolish man built his house, 'and the rain descended, and the floods came, and the winds blew, and beat upon that house; and it fell; and great was the fall of it.'

"The limpet is wiser. It never trusts to the shifting sand, but holds firmly to the immovable rock. Be like it in resisting all attempts, whether of human or spiritual foes, to drag you from the Rock."

"Papa," said Max slowly and with some hesitation. "I wish to do so—I think it is my settled purpose, but I—I feel afraid that sometime I may let go. I'm a careless, heedless fellow, you know, and—well, I'm afraid I may forget to hold fast to Jesus and be over come by some sudden, irresistable, and great temptation."

"There is danger of that, my boy," the captain returned with feeling. "Yet I should have greater fear for you if I heard you talk in a self-confident and boasting spirit. Trusting in ourselves, we are not safe, but trusting in Jesus, we are. We are safe only while we cling to our sure foundation, the Rock, Christ Jesus. But our greatest security is in the joyful fact that He holds us fast and will never let go, if we have indeed given ourselves to Him.

"He says, 'My sheep hear My voice and I know them, and they follow Me; and I give unto them eternal life; and they shall never perish, neither shall any man pluck them out of my hand.'"

"Such sweet words of promise, papa, aren't they?" Lulu asked softly.

"Yes, words that have been an untold comfort and support to many of God's dear children on their way Zionward. The sword of the Spirit with which they have fought Satan's lying assertion that they might yet be lost in spite of having fled for refuge to Him who died on Calvary."

"Is it those words the Bible means when it speaks of the sword of the Spirit, papa?" asked Max.

"Not those alone, but all the Word of God. And in order to be prepared to wield the Word, we must hide it in our hearts. David says, 'Thy word have I hid in my heart, that I might not sin against Thee.'

"Christ is our pattern. We must strive to follow his example in all things. It was with the sword of the Spirit he repelled every temptation of the devil there in the wilderness—beginning each reply to the evil suggestions with 'It is written.'"

"That is why you have us learn so many Bible verses, papa?"

"Yes, open the Bible laying on the table there, Max, and turn to the sixth chapter of Deuteronomy."

Max did so, then read, by his father's direction, the sixth and seventh verses.

"And these words which I command thee this day, shall be in thine heart; and thou shalt teach them diligently unto thy children, and shalt talk of them when thou sittest in thine house, and when thou walkest by the way, and when thou liest down, and when thou risest up."

"I think you obey that command, papa," said Lulu. "Indeed I think you try to obey every single command in God's Word."

"I do," he replied. "And I want my children to follow my example in that. In the eleventh chapter of the same book, the command is repeated and these words are added, 'that your days may multiplied, and the days of your children, in the land which the Lord sware unto your fathers to give them, as the days of heaven upon the earth.'

"Speaking of the law, the testimony, the statutes, the commandments of the Lord, the psalmist tells us that 'in keeping of them is great reward.'

"True happiness is known by none but those who are at peace with God. But living in the light of His countenance, one may be full of joy even in the midst of great earthly tribulation.

"Ah, my darlings, I can wish nothing better for you than that you may thus live!"

At that moment Violet joined them.

"The babies were both unusually wakeful and troublesome tonight," she remarked. "But they have at last fallen asleep and so released mamma from attendance upon them."

"To our great content," added her husband, gently putting Lulu off his knee and rising to give his wife a seat, but Max sprang up and gallantly placed a chair for her—selecting the most comfortable and placing it close beside his father's.

She thanked him with one of her sweetest smiles, and the captain remarked, "Max was too quick for me this time, my dear."

"Like his father, he is extremely polite and attentive to ladies," said Violet. "How cozy you are here! And you two children have been having a pleasant time, no doubt, with papa all to yourselves."

"We have missed you, my dear," said her husband. "At least, I may speak for myself."

"And we would have been glad if you could have come sooner," added Max.

"Have you all been laying plans for the fine entertainment of our expected guests who are to keep New Year's Day with us?" she asked.

"No, my dear, your help will be needed in that," replied her husband.

"Can't we have some charades again, papa?" asked Lulu.

"I see no objection," answered her father. "Provided something new can be thought of."

"*Misunderstand*, I think might do for one," Max offered as a suggestion.

"Yes, Max, I think that might be very good," Violet said. "Perhaps *madman* would do for another."

"We'll need several words for our charades, I think," said Lulu. "And a number also for the sports at Fairview."

"But fortunately we are not responsible for the entertainment there," remarked Violet pleasantly.

"No," said the captain. "I think we will dismiss thought for our own for the present. It is time for evening worship. Max, please ring for the servants."

⚘ ⚘ ⚘ ⚘ ⚘

As usual the captain went into Lulu's room for a bit of a goodnight chat with her about the time she was ready for bed.

"Papa," she said, nestling close in his arms, "I have been thinking more about the kind of year this has been for me, and I think I must always remember it as a good one because I have learned to love Jesus! I know I have done some very wrong things even since I became His servant. But, oh, papa, I do love Him and want to serve Him! How glad I am that He is so forgiving, and that He says He will never let anyone pluck me out of His hand!"

"Yes, child, it is a precious assurance, and we may rejoice in it—you and I and all of His people.

"But ever let us keep in mind and obey those other words of our blessed Master, 'Watch and pray, that ye enter not into temptation.'

"Remember that we are to be good soldiers of Jesus Christ, and that we have a great battle to fight with the evil that is in our own hearts, the snares of the world, and the powers of darkness. Satan and his hosts of wicked spirits great desire and aim is to ruin our souls and drag us down to the dreadful place prepared for them."

"Papa, sometimes I feel afraid of them," she said, shuddering. "But Jesus is stronger than any of them and won't let them hurt me if I trust in Him?"

"Stronger than all of them put together and will not let any, or all of them, pluck you out of His hand. We are safe there. In the eighth chapter of Romans we find these triumphant words. 'I am persuaded, that neither death, nor life, nor angels, nor principalities, nor powers, nor things present, nor things to come, nor height, nor depth, nor any other creature, shall be able to separate us from the love of God, which is in Christ Jesus our Lord!'"

CHAPTER ELEVENTH

IN ALL THE HOMES of the Dinsmore connection, Sunday was always a peacefully quiet day—kept as a sacred time of rest from toil and worldly cares and pleasures.

The quiet and leisure for thought were particularly pleasurable for Grandma Elsie in her pleasant home at Ion on this last Sunday of the old year.

She had enjoyed having her friends about her and seeing the hilarity of the children and youth. She was still youthful in her feelings and full of an ever-ready sympathy with the young, none of whom could know her without loving her. To all who could claim kin with her—especially her children and grandchildren—she was a person of devoted affection, affection fully reciprocated by her.

And so the frequent reunions at Ion were a source of delight to both her and them.

Yet there were times when her spirit craved exclusive companionship with her nearest and dearest. There were other seasons when she would be alone with Him whom her "soul desired above all earthly joy and earthly love."

An hour had been spent in secret communion with Him ere Rosie and Walter came for their half-hour of Bible study and prayer in mamma's dressing room before breakfast, to which they had been accustomed since their earliest recollection.

And not they only, but their older brothers and sisters before them, every one of whom had very tender memories connected with that very short service. Those memories had been a safeguard to them in times if temptation, a comfort and support in the dark hours that sooner or later come to all the sons and daughters of Adam, and made them feel it even yet a privilege to participate when circumstances would permit.

Sometimes Edward and Zoe joined in the little circle, and Harold and Herbert seldom failed to do so when at home. They all did so this morning and with an enjoyment that made the allotted time seem far too short.

Their mother had always been able to interest her children in Bible lessons.

Breakfast and family worship followed — then common attendance upon the morning service of the sanctuary.

After that there was Sunday school for the servants in the schoolhouse on the estate — the mother and all her children acting as teachers.

The afternoon and evening were given to reading, conversation, and music suited to the sacredness of the day. Then all retired to peaceful slumbers from which they rose in the morning rested and refreshed in body and mind and ready to enter with zest upon the labors and pleasures of the new week.

According to the arrangements made the previous week, the whole Ion family and all who had been guests there at that time repaired to Fairview at an early hour. There they spent the day together in social festivities similar to those with which they had enlivened their stay with Grandma Elsie.

Harold and Herbert gave a magic lantern exhibition, some charades were acted, and Cousin Ronald contrived to add not a little to the fun by timely efforts in his own particular line. The very little ones were delighted to hear their toy dogs bark, roosters crow, hens and geese cackle, ducks quack, horses neigh, and donkeys bray.

They could hardly believe that the sounds that seemed to come from the mouths of the toy animals were really made by Cousin Ronald, and when assured that such was the case, thought him a most wonderful man.

Some of the guests departed that evening, but some others remained overnight—among them the Raymond family.

On Tuesday morning, they went home to Woodburn, taking Grandma Elsie, Rosie, Walter, and Evelyn Leland with them.

Lulu had been sharing Evelyn's room at Fairview and now was to have the pleasure of returning the hospitality.

There were some preparations to be made for the entertainment of tomorrow's guests, and the children were in a flutter of pleasurable excitement.

Words can scarcely tell how much they enjoyed their share of the planning and arranging and the consultations together and with the older people, or how kindly indulgent the captain was to their wishes and fancies—never saying them nay when it was within his power to grant their request.

Evelyn Leland loved to watch Lulu and Gracie as they hung affectionately about their father, giving and receiving caresses and endearments. However, the sight often brought tears to her eyes, calling up tender memories of the past. She had not forgotten—she never could forget—the dear parent who had been wont to lavish such caresses and endearments upon her. At times, her young heart ached with its longing to hear again the sound of his voice and feel the clasp of his arm and his kisses upon cheek and lip and brow.

Yet life was gliding along very peacefully and happily with her, brightened by the love of kindred and friends, and she could join very heartily in the diversions and merriment of her companions.

Tea was over, the babies had had their romp with papa, brother, and sisters and been carried off to the nursery, leaving the rest of the family — the guests included — in the pleasant library.

"Well, my dears, it has been a busy day with you," remarked Grandma Elsie, smiling pleasantly upon the group of children. "But I presume your preparations for tomorrow's sports are quite completed now?"

"Yes, ma'am," said Lulu.

"And we have some very good charades, mamma," said Rosie. "We have also arranged for some nice tableaux."

"New ones?"

"New and old both," answered Rosie and Lulu together. "And, oh, Grandma Elsie, we want another with you in it," added Lulu with eager entreaty in her tones.

"And why with me, my dear?" asked Mrs. Travilla with a pleased little laugh. "Are there not more than enough younger people to take part?"

"Oh, there are plenty of us such as we are!" laughed Eva. "But we want all the beautiful people, so that the pictures will be beautiful."

"You are coming out in a new character, Eva, that of an adroit flatterer," returned Grandma Elsie with a look of amusement. "But I am not displeased, my dear child, because I credit it entirely to your affection, which I prize very highly," she hastened to add, seeing that her words had called up a blush of painful embarrassment on Eva's usually placid face.

"Grandma Elsie, we all love you dearly," said Lulu. "But you are beautiful. I'm sure everybody thinks so. Don't they, papa?"

"As far as my knowledge goes," he answered, smiling and pinching her cheek—for as usual, she was close at his side. "And indeed I don't know how anyone could think otherwise."

"Mamma will do it, I'm sure," said Walter. "Because we want her to, and she's always kind."

"Will what?" asked Violet, coming into the library at that moment.

"Be one in a tableau," replied Walter.

"Yes, of course," said Violet. "Oh, we'll make a group with mamma, grandpa, sister Elsie, and her little Ned and call it a picture of four generations. If dear old grandpa were with us still we could make it five."

"A very nice idea, my dear," the captain remarked with a glance of affectionate admiration at his young wife, as he rose and handed her a chair. "I think we must have the group photographed."

"Oh, yes. Lester can do it beautifully! We'll send him word to bring his apparatus with him."

"Yes," said her mother. "And we will ask him to take us all in family groups. The pictures will be pleasant mementos of this holiday season."

"Mamma," said Walter, "I think if you would tell us about all the New Year's Days you can remember, it would be a very interesting way of spending the evening."

"Yes, mamma, we would all be charmed to hear your story," said Violet. The others chiming in with "Oh, yes, mamma," "Yes, Grandma Elsie, please do tell it."

"Since you all seem to desire it, I will try," she answered kindly. "But I fear my reminiscences will hardly deserve the name of story.

"The first Christmas and New Year's of which I retain a vivid remembrance were those of the first winter after I had made the acquaintance of my dear father. As I believe you all know, I never saw him until I was eight years old.

"The occurrences of that Christmas are too familiar to most, if not to all, to bear repetition."

"But you hadn't at all a nice New Year's that time, mamma," said Rosie, softly stroking and patting the hand she held. Then she lifted it to her lips, for she was sitting on a stool at her mother's feet, while the others had grouped themselves around her. "You were suffering so with that sprained ankle."

"Ah, there you are mistaken, my child," Grandma Elsie answered with her own sweet smile. "For I had a most enjoyable day inspite of the injury that kept me a prisoner in my room. My father brought me a beautiful doll baby, quite as large as some live ones that I have seen, and a quantity of pretty things to be used in its adornment. My little friends and I had a merry, happy time cutting out garments and making them up.

"The next Christmas and New Year's Day were spent in our new home at the Oaks, which my papa had bought and furnished in the meantime.

"My Christmas gifts were beautiful—from papa books and a pearl necklace and bracelets, which are now the property of my daughter Rosie," she said, smiling down at Rosie as she spoke. "And there was a ring to match from him who was afterward my beloved husband. There were also books from his mother and my Aunt Adelaide. They were our guests at dinner that day.

"Between breakfast and dinner I had the pleasure of distributing gifts among the house servants and the Negroes at the quarter. Then I had a ride with papa, and the evening, till my early bedtime, was spent sitting on his knee."

"But you are going to tell us about that New Year's, too, mamma, aren't you?" asked Walter, as she paused in her narrative, sitting quietly with a pensive, far-off look in her soft, hazel eyes.

"Yes," she said rousing from her reverie, "I remember it was on the day after Christmas that papa asked me if I was going to make a New Year's present to each of my little friends.

"Of course, I was quite delighted with the idea, especially as he allowed me great latitude in regard to the amount to be spent."

"And did he take you to the stores and let you choose the presents, Grandma Elsie?" asked Lulu. "That would be half the fun, I think."

"My dear, indulgent father would have done so, had I been able to bear the fatigue," Grandma Elsie replied. "But at that time I was quite feeble from a severe illness. He did not think me strong enough to visit the stores. He ordered goods sent out to the Oaks for me to select from, which gave me nearly as much enjoyment as I could have found in going to the city in search of them."

"Did you find gifts to suit, mamma?" queried Walter. "Oh, won't you tell us how many of your little friends there were and what the gifts were?"

"Besides the Roselands little people," replied his mother, "there were Lucy and Herbert Carrington, Carry Howard, Isabel Carleton, Mary Leslie, and Flora Arnott to be remembered.

"For the last named, who was also the youngest, I selected a beautiful wax doll and a complete wardrobe of ready-made clothes for it—all neatly packed in a tiny trunk.

"To Mary Leslie I gave a ring, and to each of the other girls, a handsome bracelet. To Herbert, who was a great reader, I gave a set of handsomely bound books.

"All these little friends of mine were spending the Christmas holidays at Pinegrove—the home of the Howard family.

"Papa and I had been invited, too, but had declined because of my feeble state. When my gifts were ready I asked him if they should be sent to Pinegrove.

"'We will see about it,' he answered. 'We have plenty of time. There are two days yet, and it will not take a messenger half an hour to travel from here to Pinegrove.'

"So I said no more, for I never was allowed to beg.

"But when New Year's morning came, and the presents had not been sent, I began to feel decidedly uneasy. Papa evidently perceived it, though neither of us said a word on the subject that was uppermost in my mind.

"Papa had some beautiful books and pictures for me, which he gave me before breakfast, saying that he hoped they would help me pass the day pleasantly. He would be glad to make it the happiest New Year I had known yet.

"He smiled tenderly upon me as he said it, then held me close in his arms and kissed me over and over again. I returned his kisses, putting my arms about his neck and hugging him as tight as I could.

"After that we had breakfast and family worship, and then he took me on his knee again and asked how I would like to spend the day.

"I answered that I would be glad to have a drive if he did not think it too cold. He said he thought it was not if I were well wrapped up.

"There was no snow to make for sleighing, so the carriage was ordered, I was bundled up in furs, and we drove several miles.

"As we were about starting I ventured to ask, 'Papa, haven't you forgotten to send my presents to Pinegrove?' He smiled and said, 'No, my darling,' in a very pleasant tone, but that was all. When we came back I noticed that the presents were still in a closet in my dressing room where they had been ever since they were bought.

"I was quite puzzled about it but asked no questions.

"Mammy arranged my hair and dress, and I went back to the parlor where papa was sitting, reading. He laid aside his book as soon as I entered the room, took me on his knee, and began telling me funny stories that kept me laughing till a carriage drove up to the door.

"'There, someone has come!' he said. 'It seems we are not to spend the day alone after all.'

"Then, in another minute or two, the door opened and in came my six little friends for whom I had bought the presents."

Gracie clapped her hands in delight. "Oh, how nice! Didn't you have a good time, Grandma Elsie?"

"Yes, very — they had all come to spend the day. I had the pleasure of presenting my gifts in person and of seeing that they were fully appreciated. We played quiet games, and papa told us lovely stories. There was no fretting or quarrelling. Everybody was in high good humor, and when the time came to separate, my guests all bade good-bye, saying that they had never had a more enjoyable day."

"Now please tell about the next Christmas and New Year's, mamma," urged Walter as she paused. He was apparently feeling that her tale was ended.

"Let mamma have time to breathe and to think what comes next, Walter," said Rosie. "Don't you see that's what she is doing?"

"I am thinking of those little friends of mine," sighed their mother. "Asking myself, 'Where are they now?' Ah, what changes life brings! How short and hasty it is and how soon it will be over! I mean the life in this world.

"It is likened in the Bible to a pilgrimage, a tale that is told, a flower that soon withers or is cut down by the mowers scythe, a dream, a sleep, a vapor, a shadow, a handbreadth, or a thread cut by the weaver."

"Mamma, are those friends of yours all dead?" asked Walter.

"I will tell you about them, my boy," she answered. "Herbert Carrington died young — he was barely sixteen."

With the words, a look of great pain swept across the still fair, sweet face of the speaker, and she paused for a moment as if almost overcome by some sad recollection.

Violet, who had heard the story from Grandma Rose, understood it.

"Mamma, dear," she said softly, "what a happy thing it was for him—poor sufferer that he was—to be taken so early to the Father's house on high where pain and sin and sorrow are unknown!"

"Yes," returned her mother, furtively wiping away a tear. "And calling to mind the dreadful scenes of the war that followed some years later and the sore trials that resulted in the Carrington family—I feel that he was taken away from the evil to come.

"Of the others forming that little company—Flora Arnott, too, died young. Mary Leslie married and moved away, and I have lost sight of her for many years. Carry Howard lived to become a wife and mother, but she was called away from earth years and years ago. The same words would tell Isabel Carleton's story.

"Lucy Carrington and I are the only ones left. She, like myself, has children and grandchildren. I hear from her now and then, and we meet occasionally when I go North or she pays a visit to the old home at Ashlands."

"Mrs. Ross," said Rosie aloud, half in assertion, half inquiringly.

"Yes, that is her married name."

"Aunt Sophy who lives at Ashlands now is—"

"The widow of Lucy's older brother, Harry, and also your Grandma Rose's sister, as you all know."

"Mamma," said Walter, "you didn't mention Grandma Rose at all in telling your story of that Christmas and New Year's. Wasn't she there?"

"No, my son. My father—your grandpa—and I were living alone together at that time. The next summer we went North, and while there, we visited Elmgrove, Mr. Allison's country place, which gave papa and Miss Rose an opportunity to become quite well acquainted.

"I had known and loved Miss Rose before, and I was very glad when papa told me she had consented to become his wife and my mother.

"They were married in the fall, and when we returned to the Oaks, she was with us.

"That made my next Christmas and New Year still happier than the last, and when yet another came around, my treasures had been increased in number by the advent of a darling little brother."

"Uncle Horace," said Walter. "Mamma, were you very glad when God gave him to you?"

"Indeed I was!" she answered with a smile. "I had never had a brother or a sister and had often been hungry for one.

"And he has always been a dear, loving brother to me," she went on. "And your Aunt Rose, who came to us while we were in Europe some eight years later, was as sweet a sister as anyone could ever desire."

"But about those holidays, mamma, the first when you had a brother?" persisted Walter. "Aren't you going to tell about them?"

"Yes," she answered. "It was an enjoyable time, for we had our cousins—Mildred and Annis Keith—with us. Mildred, though, had become Mrs. Landreth, and her husband and baby boy were with her.

"Annis was a dear, lovable little girl just about my own age. They spent the winter at the Oaks, Annis sharing both my studies and my sports. We had a Christmas party, and our guests remained with us at the Oaks through the rest of that next week."

"Oh, mamma, do please go on and tell the whole story of that Christmas and all the good times you had that winter," pleaded Rosie. "I have always enjoyed it so much, and I'm sure Eva and Lulu and Gracie will, too."

Rosie's request was seconded by several other voices in the little crowd, and Grandma Elsie, ever willing to give pleasure, kindly complied.

All her listeners were greatly interested. Lulu gathered from it a far different impression of Mr. Dinsmore as a father from that which she had derived from tales told her by some of the old servants in the family connection.

They had given her the idea that Mr. Dinsmore was exceedingly stern and tyrannical, but his daughter painted him as a most loving and indulgent parent. Mayhap the truth lay somewhere between the two pictures, for as he himself had often said, Elsie was ever wont to look upon him through rose-colored glasses.

"You did have a very nice time, Grandma Elsie! I could almost wish I'd been in your place," exclaimed Lulu, when the tale had come to an end. "But, no, I don't either, for then I couldn't be my father's child," putting her cheek to his. "And to belong to him is better than anything else!"

"My little Lulu as the judge," laughed the captain, tightening the clasp of his arm about her waist.

"Or any other of your children," added Gracie from her seat on his knee, affectionately stroking his face with her small, white hand as she spoke. "Grandma Elsie, won't you please go on and tell about other Christmases that you remember?"

"I think, my dear, I have done my full share of storytelling for one evening," replied Mrs. Travilla pleasantly. "It is your father's turn now, as the next in age. Captain, will you not favor us with some of your reminiscences of former holiday experiences, or something else, if you prefer. I know you are a famous storyteller."

"Oh, yes, captain!" "Oh, yes, papa, do, please," urged the others.

"Some other time, perhaps," he said. "Do you know how late it is? It's time to call the servants in to prayers, and then for the little folks to seek their nests. Max, my son, please ring the bell."

"Then you don't mean to let us stay up to watch the old year out and the new year in, papa?" queried the lad as he rose and obeyed the order.

"Hardly," his father answered with a slight smile. "You are all too young to be allowed to lose so large a portion of your night's rest. To do so would spoil all the anticipated pleasure of tomorrow."

"Then I am sure we don't want to, captain," said Evelyn. "For we are looking forward to a great deal of pleasure."

CHAPTER TWELFTH

"MY LITTLE GRACIE looks very, very tired," the captain said, bending down and taking her in his arms as the little folks were bidding goodnight. "I shall carry you upstairs, darling, after the old custom."

"Thank you, papa. I'm very willing," replied Gracie, clasping his neck with her small arms.

"Lulu, shall I say goodnight to you first?" he asked, smiling down at his eldest daughter, who was standing by his side. "Because you have Eva with you, you will perhaps not care for the usual bit of goodnight chat with your father?"

"Yes, indeed I do care for it, papa!" cried Lulu. "Why, I sha'n't have another chance this year! I wouldn't miss it for anything!"

"Then you shall not," he said, looking both pleased and amused. "That sounds as though the next opportunity were far in the distance."

He passed out the room as he spoke and went on up the wide stairway, Lulu and Eva following, each with an arm about the other's waist.

"Those talks must be so delightful," remarked the latter in a low tone and with a slight sigh. "I'm very glad you don't let me hinder them, dear Lu."

"I knew you wouldn't want me to," said Lulu. "You are always so kind and thoughtful for others, and though papa sometimes give me a quarter of an hour or more when we have a great deal to say to each other, I think he won't stay more than a minute or two tonight! It won't keep me long away from you."

"Oh, please, don't hurry for my sake," said Eva. She added softly, "You know I, too, shall be glad of a few minutes alone with my best Friend. So if you like, I will go into the little tower room while your papa is with you."

"You can have both that and my bedroom to yourself, dear," returned Lulu. "I shall receive papa in the little sitting room that is Gracie's and mine."

They had reached the upper hall. The captain passed into Gracie's bedroom and Lulu into her own, Eva with her.

"Such a sweet, pretty room!" Eva said, glancing around it. "I am always struck with the thought on coming into it, though I have seen it so often."

"Yes," returned Lulu, her face lighting up with pleasure. "I think it so myself. Our dear father is constantly adding pretty things here and there to our rooms, and doing so much to make his children happy! Yet, would you believe it, Eva? I am sometimes both ill-tempered and disobedient to him."

"Not now! Not lately?" Evelyn said in assertion and with a look of surprise.

"Yes," Lulu replied in a low, remorseful tone, her eyes downcast, her face flushing painfully. "Only last month. One day Max was teasing me, and I was in very bad humor, so answered him crossly. Papa happened to be in the next room and overheard it all, and he called us both to come to him. His voice sounded stern, and I felt angry and rebellious. Max never does feel so, I believe. Anyway, he's always obedient, and he went at once, but I waited to be called a second time, and—oh, Eva, I'm dreadfully, dreadfully ashamed! But I feel as if I must tell you because I can't bear to have you think me so much better than I am."

"Dear Lu, don't tell it if it hurts you so. I'm sure if you were not a good girl you wouldn't feel so very sorry and ashamed," Evelyn interrupted, putting both arms around her friend and kissing her with warmth and affection.

"No, indeed, I'm not!" said Lulu. "And I'll tell it, if only to punish myself for my badness. Papa has never punished me for it, though I really wish he would and asked him to over and over again."

"That seems very odd," Eva said, smiling. "Most people are only too glad to escape punishment."

"Maybe I'm different from most folks," said Lulu. "But I have always want to beat myself when I've been so hateful. So if papa punishes me, I always feel a good deal happier after it's over.

"But I must finish my story. Papa asked, 'Lulu did you hear me bid you come to me?' and I answered, 'Yes, sir,' then muttered, 'but I'll not come a step till I get ready.'"

Evelyn seemed lost in astonishment. "Oh, Lu! Did you really say that? How could you even venture to speak so to your father—a man whom everybody respects so highly and who is so dear and kind to you?"

"I did," acknowledged Lulu, her head hanging still lower and her cheek flushing more hotly. "You see when I lived with Aunt Beulah I got into the way of being very saucy with her, and I suppose that's how I came to speak so to papa. Oh, don't you think I ought to be dreadfully ashamed, and that papa should have punished me very severely?"

"I suppose he is the best judge of that," Eva answered doubtfully. "But what did he do? Surely he didn't pass over it as of no consequence? I think he wouldn't feel it right to allow his own child to refuse obedience to his commands."

"No, of course not. The minute I said the words I could have bitten my tongue off for it. I hoped papa hadn't heard, but he had. He rose from his chair and came toward me—very quietly, not at all as if he were in a passion—and I jumped up, saying, 'I will, papa. I'm coming.'

"Then he said in a tone as if he were grieved and astonished that his own little girl could talk so to him, 'Tardy obedience following upon a most insolent refusal to obey,' and took my hand and led me to the side of his chair.

"Then he sat down and talked to Max a little and sent him up to his room. After Max had gone he talked to me.

"He said that he must punish me, but he would try a new way. For four days, I shouldn't be his child at all—at least not to be treated like it, but just as if I were a little girl visitor. He wouldn't give me any orders or advice or direction or instruction, and I mustn't take any liberties with him that I wouldn't feel free to take with a stranger gentleman.

"He said I must understand that he did not intend to subject me to any harsh treatment, but he would be as polite and attentive to my wants as if I were a guest in the house."

"Oh, Lu, did you like it? Was it nice?"

"No, indeed! I thought they were the longest four days I'd ever lived, and I wondered how I could ever have thought I'd like to be my own mistress instead of having to obey papa.

"He didn't give me one cross word or even a look, but he didn't invite me to sit on his knee, and I didn't dare do so. He didn't call me pet names and hug me up in his arms, as he so often does when I haven't been naughty. I couldn't wait on him as I always love to do. He wouldn't let me do the least thing for him. I just felt as if I weren't one of the family at all, and I would ten times rather have had the hardest of whippings—at least so far as the pain was concerned."

"Yes, of course. It wouldn't have been half so hard to bear. At least I can imagine that to be made to feel yourself only a stranger in your father's house would be a great deal worse than having to endure quite severe bodily pain. So I think you may feel that you have been punished."

"Not so severely as I deserved," returned Lulu, shaking her head and sighing. "No, not half. There, I can hear Gracie calling me to say good-night. Excuse me while I run into her room for a few minutes."

She found Gracie alone and just getting into bed.

"Where's papa?" Lulu asked.

"Gone downstairs, but he said he'd be back in a few minutes to have his bit of chat with you in the sitting room."

"Then, I'll just kiss you goodnight and hurry back to get ready for him."

When the captain came, he found Lulu ready and waiting for him, seated by the fire with her Bible open in her hand.

"I was learning my verse for tomorrow morning, papa." she said, closing the Book and laying it aside, as she rose to give him the easy chair she had been occupying.

"That was right," he replied, sitting down and drawing her to his knee. "One could hardly end the old year or begin the new in a better way than by the study of God's Word. Well, has my little daughter anything particular to say to her father tonight?"

"Only that I wish I'd been a better daughter to you, papa, and that I hope I shall be this—no, next year, the year that's to begin in a few hours. I do hope that when its last night comes, you can say, 'My daughter Lulu hasn't been once disobedient or in a passion for a whole year.'"

"It would be a very happy thing for me—for us both—if I can," he said. "And I am not without hope that it may be so. But, my dear child, you will need constant watchfulness lest your besetting sins overcome you when you least expect it."

"I wish I could get done with the fight," she sighed. "It's such a hard one."

"Yes, I know, dear child, for I am engaged in the same conflict. But we must keep on resolutely till the dear Master calls us home.

"But we have the promise of His help all the way, and that we shall be 'more than conquerors through Him that loved us.' And the prize is eternal life at God's right hand."

"Will it be always easy to be good when we get to heaven?"

"Yes, the last remains of the old, evil nature will have been taken away, and we will have no more inclination to sin."

"I am very glad of that! And I am glad that God gave me such a good Christian father to help me in my hard fight! And, papa, I must tell you again that I am very, very sorry and ashamed because of my naughtiness last month."

"Dear child, my dear, humble, penitent little girl!" he said tenderly. "It has long since been fully and freely forgiven. Now goodnight, my darling, and good-bye till next year," he added in playful tone, kissing her fondly over and over again. "That is unless something unforeseen should make you want your father before morning. In that case you will not have far to run to find him."

"Oh, no, and it makes me glad always at night to remember that you are so near and the doors are all open between our rooms, so that you could hear me if I should call out to you, papa. I know you wouldn't be displeased at being awakened if I were in trouble and needed you."

"No, indeed, daughter. In that case I should be only too glad to be roused that I might hasten to your assistance.

"But let your greatest rejoicing be in the thought that you and I and all of us are under the care of Him who neither slumbers nor sleeps. 'It is better to trust in the Lord than to put confidence in man.'"

Rosie in her mamma's room, which she shared at this time, as on a former occasion, was preparing for bed. Grandma Elsie was quietly reading in an easy chair beside the fire.

Presently Rosie went to the side of the chair and dropped on her knees, looking up smilingly into the sweet, placid face bent over the book.

"Mamma, dear, I have come for my goodnight kiss before getting into bed," she said softly. "The last I shall solicit from you this year."

"And you are going to be satisfied with one?" her mother asked, letting the book fall into her lap, while she laid one hand gently on her young daughter's head and gazed tenderly down into the blooming face. "What a sad expression she wears," Rosie thought.

"I say no to that, mamma," she returned, laying her head in her mother's lap and taking into her own the hand that had been resting on it, to press it again and again to her lips with ardent affection, "for I shall not be satisfied with less than half a dozen of your kisses."

Elsie gave them in quick succession, gathering her child in her arms and making her rest her fair head on the maternal bosom. Rosie felt a warm tear fall on her cheek.

"Mamma!" she exclaimed in concerned surprise. "You are crying! What can be the matter? Have I said or done anything to grieve your dear heart?" She reached an arm up to clasp her mother's neck, while she scanned the loved features with earnest, tender scrutiny.

For a minute or more there was no reply. Then Elsie said, in moved tones, softly smoothing the hair back from Rosie's temples as she spoke and gazing tenderly down into her eyes, "My heart is sad for you, my darling, because, while another year is rapidly drawing to a close, I have yet no reason to hope that you have sought a refuge within the fold of the good Shepherd who gives to his sheep eternal life. The dear Saviour who has been inviting you to come to Him and be saved."

"Mamma, I am very young yet," murmured Rosie, hanging her head and blushing.

"Old enough to have become a disciple of Jesus years ago," her mother said in sorrowful tones. "Oh, my darling, give Him the best years of your life—the whole of your life, whether it be long or short. Is He not worthy of it?"

"Yes, mamma, surely there can be only one answer to that, and I do mean to—to try to turn over a new leaf with the coming of the new year. But, mamma, I know of a number of good Christians who didn't begin to be such till they were many years older than I am. There is grandpa for one."

"Yes, my child," sighed her mother. "But he has always deeply regretted having so long delayed beginning the Christian course, entering the service of the dear Master whom now he loves better than wife or child or any created being. There are many reasons, my darling, why delay is both dangerous and unwise as well as basely ungrateful."

"You allude to the uncertainty of life, mamma?"

"Yes, and of the continuance of both health and reason. How many have been suddenly overtaken by fatal illness that at once robbed them of the power to think, and if preparation for the solemn realities of another world had not been already made, the opportunity for so doing was forever lost!

"There is also danger that God's Spirit may cease to strive with you, and without His help, you can never come to Christ.

"Nor do we know how soon Jesus may come again in the clouds of heaven. He himself has told us that He will come as a thief in the night—that is, when He is not expected.

"But, Rosie, my dear child, even if you could know certainly that delay will not cost you the loss of your soul, it will bring you another loss both great and irreparable."

"What, mamma?" Rosie asked with a look of mingled surprise and alarm. "I cannot think what you mean."

"While it is a precious truth that all who finally repent and accept of Christ as their only Saviour will inherit eternal life—a life of holiness and unspeakable happiness at God's right hand," answered her mother. "There will be a difference in the portions of those who have spent many years in the faithful service of the Master, using their time and talents for the advancement of His cause and kingdom and striving to win others to know and serve Him, as they themselves grow in grace and conformity to His likeness and His will and that of others who have been saved only at the last and so by fire. All will be perfectly happy but some will have a greater capacity for happiness than others.

"According to the teachings of God's word, sin is the greatest folly, and the service of God the highest wisdom.

"'Doth not wisdom cry and understanding put forth her voice? Riches and honor are with me; yea, durable riches and righteousness. My fruit is better than gold, yea, than fine gold; and my revenue than choice silver!

"'They that be wise shall shine as the brightness of the firmament; and they that turn many to righteousness, as the stars forever and ever.'

"Rosie, my darling, it is the dearest wish of my heart to see you engaged in that work, but you cannot teach others what you do not know yourself. You must first give your heart to God and learn for yourself the sweetness of His love. Will you not do it now, at once? Oh, listen to His gracious invitation, 'Give Me thine heart.'"

For some moments, a deep and solemn hush seemed to fill the room, Rosie kneeling there with her head pillowed on her mother's breast, Elsie's heart going up in an almost agonizing petition for her child.

At length Rosie lifted her head, looking up into her mother's face with dewy eyes and a very sweet smile.

"Mamma," she said in low tremulous tones, "I have tried to do it. I have asked the Lord to forgive my sins, to cleanse me from mine iniquities, and to take me for His very own. I think He has heard and granted my petition.

"You know when the leper came to Him saying, 'Lord, if thou wilt, thou canst make me clean,' Jesus at once put forth his hand and touched him saying, 'I will; be thou clean.' Immediately the leprosy departed from him. Mamma, I have been praying the leper's prayer, and I think the dear Lord Jesus has said the same words to me."

"I am sure of it," Elsie said with emotion. "For He is the unchangeable God, 'Jesus Christ the same yesterday, and today, and forever.' He is as ready to be moved with compassion for a sin-sick soul today as He was for the leper when on earth. And He has said, 'Him that cometh to Me I will in no wise cast out.'"

Clasping her hands and looking upward, "'Bless the Lord, oh my soul!'" she exclaimed. "'And all that is within me, bless His holy name!'"

CHAPTER THIRTEENTH

"LU! LU! FIVE O'CLOCK, time to get up!" called a harsh voice in loud, shrill tones.

"Who, who was calling?" asked Eva, starting out of sleep.

"Only Polly," laughed Lulu.

"Get up, get up, get up!" screamed the bird. "Time for breakfast. Polly wants her coffee. Polly wants a cracker."

"What a smart parrot! How plainly she talks," said Eva.

"Yes, but so loud. I'm afraid she will wake everybody in the house."

"How has she learned your name so soon?" asked Eva.

"I don't think she has," said Lulu. "Papa says there was a girl named Louisa in the place where Polly used to live that everybody called Lu, and the parrot learned to call her so, too."

"Happy New Year!" screamed Polly.

"Oh, just hear her!" cried Lulu in delight. "Papa must have been teaching her that, or having somebody else do it, while we were away. I think she's going to make a great deal of fun for us all. Happy New Year to you, Eva, dear," giving her friend a hug, as they lay side by side in the bed.

"The same to you, dear Lu," returned Eva. "How nice it is to be here with you on this easy couch with this down cover and these soft blankets over us. I've never lain on a more delightful bed. Everything about it is beautiful and luxurious, too."

"Papa was very particular to get the very best springs and mattresses for all our beds," replied Lulu. "Oh, but he is a dear, good father, always careful for the comfort and happiness of all his children!"

"And of his wife?"

"Oh, yes, indeed! I'm quite sure no man could take better care of his wife, or be more loving and kind to her, than papa is to Mamma Vi. And I'm pretty sure he was just the same to my mother. He says he loved her very dearly and loves his children—I mean Max and Gracie and me—because they were hers as well as because they are his very own."

"Lu! Lu! Get up! Time for breakfast!" screamed Polly again.

"I suppose it must be morning, or she wouldn't be making such a fuss," said Lulu.

"Yes," said Eva. "I see a little light coming in at the window."

"I'll light the gas in the sitting room and give her a cracker to stop her screaming," said Lulu, getting out of bed and feeling about for her warm slippers and dressing gown. "Then I'll run and catch papa and Gracie."

"Lulu," the captain's voice came from Gracie's room.

"I'm here, papa. Oh, a Happy New Year to you!"

"Thank you, dear child. I wish you the same, but I want you to give Polly a cracker as quickly as you can to stop her screaming. I fear she will wake both guests and babies."

"Yes, sir, I will. I was just going to," replied the little girl. "Then shall I stay up?"

"I think you may as well go back to bed and try to take another nap," he answered. "It is very, very early yet."

Lulu hurried into the sitting room where Polly's cage was hanging and struck a light.

"What you 'bout? Where you been?" demanded the parrot.

"Sleeping in my bed as I have a right to, Miss Saucebox," returned Lulu, laughing as she opened a cupboard door and brought out a paper of crackers. "There, take that and see if you can hold your tongue till folks are ready to get up."

The bird took the offered cracker and began eating it, standing on one foot on its perch and holding the food in the claws of the other, while it bit off a little at a time, Lulu looking on with interest.

"You'll have to behave better than this, or you'll be banished to the attic or the kitchen or some other far off place," she said, shaking her finger quite threateningly at Polly.

Then, after turning down the light, she ran back to bed.

"Are you asleep, Eva?" she asked in a whisper.

"No, dear, wide awake."

"Then let's talk, for I'm wide awake as can be."

"But didn't your father say you were to try for another nap?"

"I understood him to mean only that I might if I chose, not that I must. But perhaps he meant that he wanted me to, so I'll keep quiet and try."

She did so, saying to herself, "I just know it's no use, for I was never wider awake in my life." But to her astonishment the next thing she knew it was broad daylight, and Eva was up and brushing her hair before the mirror over the bureau.

"Why, I've been asleep, and I hadn't the least idea of such a thing!" cried Lulu, springing out upon the floor and beginning to dress in all haste.

"Oh, you've had a nice nap and will feel all the better for it all day, I'm sure," returned Eva laughing in a kindly way. "And that is your reward for trying to do as your papa probably wished you to. But need you hurry so? Isn't it a good while to breakfast time?"

"Yes, but I have to dress and say my prayers. And I always like so much to have a little time to chat with papa before the bell rings."

"Lu! Lu!" screamed the parrot. "Time for breakfast! Polly wants her coffee."

"Just hear Polly," exclaimed Lulu. "It does seem as if she must have sense. I suppose she does think it's time for breakfast."

"Does she drink coffee?" asked Eva.

"Yes, she is very fond of it. She gets a cup every single morning."

"She's a very amusing pet, I think," remarked Evelyn. "What fun it will be to teach her to say all sorts of cute things!"

"Yes," sighed Lulu. "But papa says if she should hear angry, passionate, or willful words from my lips she may learn and repeat them to my shame and sorrow. But, oh, I hope I never shall let her hear such!"

"I don't believe you ever will say such words any more, dear Lu," Eva said with an affectionate look into her friend's face. "I don't believe you have ever been in a passion since—since the time little Elsie had that sad fall."

"No, I have not been in a rage, but I have said some angry words a few times, and, oh—as you must remember that I told you—some very rebellious and insolent ones to my dear papa not so long ago. Oh, dear, I'm afraid my tongue can never be tamed!

"Papa made me learn that third chapter of James that says 'the tongue is a fire, a world of iniquity and that no man can tame it.' Then he talked to me so nicely and kindly about learning to rule my tongue and make it always speak as it ought—wise, kind, pleasant words. And he told me the only way to do it was by getting my heart right—by God's help—because, as the Bible tells us in another place, it is out of the abundance of the heart that the mouth speaketh."

"Your father takes a great deal of pains to teach and help you, dear Lu, doesn't he?" said Eva.

"Yes, yes, indeed!" returned Lulu with warmth. "All his children, but especially me. I think, because I'm the naughtiest and have the hardest work trying to be good. I'm often surprised at papa's patience with me and the trouble he takes to help me in my hard fight with my passionate, willful temper."

Just then Gracie's voice was heard at the door. "Happy New Year, Eva and Lu! May I come in?"

"Yes, come. Happy New Year to you," cried both girls, Lulu running and taking her sister in her arms to hug and kiss her.

"You darling child! You look bright and well. Are you, Gracie?"

"Yes, you old woman," laughed Gracie, returning the hug and kisses. "I'm all ready for breakfast. Are you?"

"No, not quite."

"I am," said Eva. "Shall we go into the sitting room, Gracie, and wait there for Lu?"

"Yes," answered Gracie, leading the way. "And I'll be learning my Bible verse while we wait for her and papa and the breakfast bell."

Lulu and her father joined the two girls at the same moment.

The captain kissed the little girls all around and presented each with a pretty portmounaie.

Eva thanked him with smiles, blushes, and very appreciative words, and his own two thanked him with hugs and kisses in addition to thanks given in words.

"Mine's ever so pretty, papa," Lulu said, turning it about in her hands.

"I am glad you are pleased with it," he said, smiling. "But are you going to be satisfied with looking at the outside? Don't you want to examine the lining also?"

"Why, yes, sir," opening it. "Oh, oh, it isn't empty!" she laughed, beginning to take out the contents—two, clean, crisp, one-dollar notes, and a handful of bright new quarters, dimes, and five-cent pieces. "Papa, how kind and generous you are to me!"

Gracie had her purse open by this time and found it lined in like manner with Lulu's. "Dear papa, thank you ever so much," she said, looking up into his face with eyes full of love and gratitude. "It's a great deal for me to have beside all the rest you gave me."

"You are both as welcome as possible, my darlings. Only make good use of it, remembering that money is one of the talents for which we must give account to God for at the last," he answered to both.

"Eva, my dear," turning to her, "you will find the same in yours, and I hope will accept it from me as though you were one of my daughters. Do me the kindness of letting me be in some respects a father to you, since your own is absent here and now but is in the happy home to which I trust we are all traveling."

She was standing near, the present he had given in her hand. She had been looking from it to Lulu and Gracie, thinking the while how good it was of the captain to treat her so much like one of his own. Now at these kind words spoken in tender fatherly tones, both heart and eyes grew full to overflowing.

He saw that she could not speak for emotion, and taking her hand, he drew her to his knee and kissed her, saying, "Don't try to thank me in words, my dear. Your speaking countenance tells me all you would say."

"What you 'bout?" screamed Polly at that instant, just as if she were calling the captain to account for his actions.

That made them all laugh—even Evelyn, who had just been ready to cry. Then the breakfast bell rang and everybody hastened to obey its summons. Many a "Happy New Year" was exchanged among them as they gathered—a bright-faced, cheerful set—in the pleasant breakfast room and about its bountiful table.

Each had a gift to show, for all had been remembered in that way by either the captain or Violet, some by both, and each one had received or did now receive something from Grandma Elsie—a book, toy, or game.

The gifts seemed to give universal satisfaction and all were in merriest spirits.

Shortly after breakfast, almost before the children had finished with comparing and talking about their presents, the other guests began to arrive, and by ten o'clock everybody who had been invited was there.

Then began the fun of arranging themselves in groups and having photographs taken and after that the acting of the charades.

The picture suggested by Violet was taken first. In it Grandma Elsie was seated between her father on one side and her namesake daughter on the other. Mrs. Leland had her babe in her arms, while little Ned leaned confidingly against his great-grandfather's knee.

The captain and Violet with their two little ones made another pretty picture. Then the captain was taken again with his older three grouped about him. Then Grandma Elsie again with her son Edward and his Zoe, standing behind her, Rosie and Walter one on each side.

She thought this quite enough, but her college boys insisted on having her taken again, seated between them.

It was then proposed that the other members of the company should be taken in turn—singly or in groups—but all declined, expressing a decided preference for spending the time in a more amusing manner, such as forming tableaux and acting out charades.

The older people took possession of a large parlor and sat there conversing, while the younger ones consulted together and made their arrangements in the library.

Misconstrue was the first word chosen. Presently Evelyn walked into the parlor, followed almost immediately by Harold with a book in his hand.

"You are here, Miss?" he said glancing at Evelyn. "And you, Miss?" as Sydney came tripping in from the hall.

"Yes, and here comes another miss," she replied as Lulu appeared in the open doorway.

"I, too, am a miss. There are four of us here now," said Rosie, coming up behind Lulu.

"And I am a miss," proclaimed Maud Dinsmore, stepping in after Rosie.

"And I am a miss," echoed Lora Howard, coming after her.

"Well, stand in a row and let us see if you can say you lesson without a miss," said Harold.

"Oh, it's a spelling school—all of girls!" remarked Gracie in a low aside to her little friend Rosie Lacey—they two having chosen a place among the spectators rather than with the actors on this occasion.

"Yes," returned Rosie. "I wonder why they don't have some of the boys in the class, too."

"When did Columbus discover America, Miss Maud?" asked Harold.

"In 1942," returned Maud with the air of one who is quite confident of the correctness of her reply.

"A miss for you," said Harold. "Next. When did Columbus discover America?"

"In 1620, just after the landing of the pilgrims," answered Sydney.

"Another miss," said Harold. "Next."

"I know that something happened in 1775," said Eva meditatively.

"Oh!" cried Rosie, "Columbus's discovery was long before that—somewhere about the year 100, was it not, Mr. Travilla?"

"A miss for each of you," replied Harold, shaking his head. "What year was it, Lulu?"

"It must have been before I was born," she answered slowly, as if not entirely certain. "Yes, I'm quite sure it was, and I can't remember before I was born."

"A miss for you, too," said Harold. "You have every one missed and will have to con your task over again."

At that each girl opened a book which she held in her hand, and for several minutes they all seemed to be studying diligently.

"Ah, ha! Ah ha! Um h'm! Mis-con" murmured Cousin Ronald, half aloud. "Vara weel done, lads and lasses. What's the next syllable? Strue? Ah ha, um, h'm! We shall see presently," as the books were closed and the young actors vanished through the door into the hall.

They were hardly gone when Zoe entered, carrying a small basket filled with flowers which she began to strew here and there over the floor.

"Ah ha! Ah ha! Um h'm!" cried Cousin Ronald. "She strews the flowers; *misconstrue* is the word, na doot."

"Ah, Cousin Ronald, somebody must have told you," laughed Zoe, tripping from the room.

"Oh!" cried Rosey Lacey. "I see now why the boys didn't take part this time—because they couldn't be miss."

"Here they come now, boys and girls, too," exclaimed Gracie. "Why, how they're laughing! I wonder what's the joke?"

They were all laughing as at something very amusing and after entering the room, did nothing but sit or stand about laughing all the time—fairly shaking with laughter, laughing, laughing till the tears came into their eyes, and the older people joined in without in the least knowing the exciting cause of so much mirth.

"Come, children, tell us the joke," said Mr. Dinsmore at length.

"Oh, grandpa, can't you see?" asked Rosie Travilla, and they all hurried from the room to return presently in a procession, each carrying something in his or her hand.

Harold had a log of wood, Herbert a post, Max a block, Frank the wooden part of an old musket, while Chester, though empty-handed, wore an old-fashioned stock or cravat and held his head very stiffly.

Maud, dressed as a huckster, had a basket filled with apples, oranges, nuts, and candies. Sydney, wearing an old cloak and straw hat, had a basket on her arm in which were needles, tapes, buttons, pins, and other small wares such as often hawked about the streets.

Lulu and Eva brought up the rear, carrying the parrot and Gracie's kitten.

Maud and Sydney made the circuit of the room, the one crying, "Apple and oranges! Buy any apples and oranges?" The other asking, "Want any pins today? Needles, buttons, shoe strings?"

"No," said Grandma Rose "Have you nothing else to offer?"

"No'm, this is my stock in trade," replied Sydney.

"I laid in a fresh stock of fruit this morning, ma'am, and it's good enough for anybody," sniffed Maud with an indignant air.

"What do you call that? A musket, sir?" asked Chester of Frank.

"No, sir, I call it the stock of one."

"Lulu and Eva, why bring those creatures in here?" asked Herbert, elevating his eyebrows as in great astonishment.

"Because they're our livestock," replied Lulu.

Now Frank began to play the part of a clown or buffoon, acting in a very silly and stupid manner, while the others looked on laughing and pointing their fingers at him in derision.

"Frank, can't you behave yourself?" exclaimed Maud. "It mortifies me to see you making yourself the laughing stock of the whole company."

"Laughing stock—laughing stock," said several voices among the spectators, and the captain added, "Very well done, indeed!"

"Thank you, sir," said Harold. "If the company are not tired, we will give them one more."

"Let us have it," said his grandfather.

Some of the girls now joined the spectators, while Harold drew out a little stand, and he, Chester, and Herbert seated themselves about it with paper and pencils before them, assuming a very businesslike air.

Frank had stepped out into the hall. In a minute or two he returned and walked up to the others, hat in hand.

Bowing low, but awkwardly, "You're the school committee, I understand, gents?" he inquired.

"Yes," said Harold. "And we want a teacher for the school at Sharon. Have you come to apply for the situation?"

"Yes, sir, I heered tell ye was wantin' a superior kind o' male man to take the school for the winter, and bein' as I was out o' a job, I thought I mout as well try my hand at that as enny thin' else."

"Take a seat and let us inquire into your job qualifications," said Herbert, waving his hand in the direction of a vacant chair. "But first tell us your name and where you are from."

"My name, sir, is Peter Bones, and I come from the town o' Hardtack in the next county—jest beyant the hill yander. I've a good eddication o' me own, too, though I never rubbed my back agin a colleg," remarked the applicant, sitting down and tilting his chair back on its hind legs and retaining his balance by holding on to the one occupied by Herbert. "I kin spell the spellin' book right straight through, sir, from kiver to kiver."

"But spelling is not the only branch to be taught in the Sharon School," said Chester. "What else do you know?"

"The three R's, sir—reading, 'riting, and 'rithmetic."

"You are acquainted with mathematics?"

"Well, no, not so much with Mathy as with his brother Bill. But I know him like a book—fact I might say like several books."

"Like several books?" echoed Chester in a sarcastic tone. "But how well may you be acquainted with the books? What's the meaning of pathology?"

"The science of road making, of course, sir. Enny fool could answer such a question as that."

"Could he, indeed? Well, you've made a miss, for your answer is wide of the mark."

"How wide is the Atlantic Ocean?" asked Herbert of the applicant.

"'Bout a thousand miles."

"Another miss—it's three thousand."

"I know it useter to be, years ago, but they've got to crossin' it so quick now that you needn't tell me it's more'n a thousand."

"Tell me, in what year was the Declaration of Independence signed?" asked Harold.

"Wall now, I don't jist remember," returned the applicant, thrusting both hands deep into his pockets and gazing down meditatively at the carpet. "Somewheres 'bout 1860, wuzn't it? No, come to think, I guess 'twas '63."

"No, no, no! You are thinking of the proclamation of emancipation. Another miss. We don't find you qualified for the situation; so we wish you good day, sir."

"Ah, ah! Ah, ah! Um, h'm, um h'm! So I should say," soliloquized Mr. Lilburn leaning on his gold-headed cane and watching the four lads as they scattered and left the room. "So this is the end of the first act, I suppose. Miss, miss, miss, ah, that's the syllable that begins the new word."

Evelyn now came in with an umbrella in her hand, Gracie and Rosey Lacey walking a little in her rear. Evelyn raised the umbrella and turning to the little girls, said pleasantly, "Come under, children, I can't keep the rain off you unless you are under the umbrella." They accepted the invitation, and the three moved slowly back and forth across the room several times.

"It's a nice sort of shelter to be under when it rains," remarked Rose Lacey.

"Yes, I like to be under it," said Gracie.

"But it is wearisome to walk all the time. Let us stand still for a little," proposed Evelyn.

"Yes, by the stand yonder," said Gracie.

They went to it and stationed themselves there for a moment, but then Gracie stepped from under the umbrella and seated herself on the carpet under the stand.

"Look, look, look!" laughed Rosie Lacey. "There's Miss Gracie Raymond under the stand—a miss-under-stand."

A storm of applause and cries of, "Well done, little ones! Very prettily done, indeed!" Gracie, rosy with blushes, came out from her retreat and ran to hide her face on her father's shoulder, while he held her close with one arm, softly smoothing her curls with the other hand.

"Don't be disturbed, darling," he said. "It is only a kind commendation of the way in which Rosie and you have acted your parts."

"Why, you should feel proud and happy, Gracie," said Zoe, drawing near. "We are going to have that tableau now in which you are to be a little flower girl. So come, won't you, and let me dress you?"

Tableaux filled the rest of the morning.

After dinner Harold and Herbert both gave a fantastic exhibition of tricks and legerdemain, which even the older people found interesting and amusing. The little ones were particularly delighted with a marvelous shower of candy that ended the performance.

After tea, some of Cousin Ronald's stories of the heroes of Scottish history and song made the evening pass delightfully.

But at an early hour the whole company, led by Grandpa Dinsmore, united in a short service of prayer, praise, and reading of the Scriptures. At its close the guests bade good-bye and scattered to their homes.

"Well," said Max, following the rest of the family into the parlor after they had seen the last guest depart, "I never had a pleasanter New Year's day."

"Nor I, either," said Lulu. "We had such a delightful time last year, too. I really don't know which I enjoyed the most."

"And we have good times all the time since we have a home of our own with our dear father in it," remarked Gracie, taking his hand and carrying it to her lips, while her sweet azure eyes looked up lovingly into his face.

An emphatic endorsement of that sentiment came from both Max and Lulu. Then the captain, smiling tenderly upon them said, "I dearly love to give you pleasure, my darlings. My heart's desire is for my children's happiness in this world and the next. But life cannot be all play, so lessons must be taken up again tomorrow morning, and I hope to find you all in an industrious and tractable mood."

"I should hope so, indeed, papa," returned Max. "If we are not both obedient and industrious, we will deserve to be called an ungrateful set."

CHAPTER
FOURTEENTH

THE WEATHER THE next day was so mild and pleasant that Max and Lulu asked and obtained permission to take a ride of several miles on their ponies.

They went alone, their father and Violet having driven out in the family carriage and taken the three younger children with them.

On their return Max and his sister approached the house from a rear entrance to the grounds, passing through a bit of woods belonging to the estate, the garden and shrubbery and across the lawn.

In traversing the wood they came upon a man leaning idly against a tree. He held himself in a lounging attitude with his hands in his pockets, a half-consumed cigar in his mouth.

He was a stranger to the children, and from his shabby, soiled clothing, unkempt locks, and unshaven face, it was evident he belonged to the order of tramps.

He stood directly in the path the children were traversing, just where it made a sudden turn, and Lulu's pony had almost trodden upon his foot before they were aware of his vicinity.

Fairy shied, snorting with fright, and almost unseated her young rider.

"Look out there and don't ride a fellow down!" growled the man, catching hold of Fairy's bridle and scowling into the face of her rider.

Lulu did not seem to be frightened. Her quick temper rose at the man's insolence, and she exclaimed authoritatively, "Let go of my bridle this instant and get out of the path."

"I will when I get ready and no sooner," returned the man insolently.

"What are you doing on these grounds, sir?" demanded Max. Then adding, he said, "You have no call to he here. Let go of that bridle and step out of the path at once."

"I'm not under your orders, bubby," said the tramp with a disagreeable, mocking laugh.

"These are my father's grounds," said Max, drawing himself up with a determined air. "And we don't allow tramps and loafers here. So, if you don't let go of the bridle and be off, I'll set my dog on you. Here, Prince, Prince!"

At the sound of the call, answered by a loud bark, and the sight of Prince's huge form making rapid bounds in his direction, the tramp released Fairy's bridle. Growling out an oath, he turned and made his way with all celerity toward the public road, leaping the fence that separated it from Captain Raymond's grounds barely in time to escape Prince's teeth as he made a dash to seize him by the leg.

"Oh!" cried Lulu, drawing a long breath of relief. "What a happy thing that Prince came running out to meet us!"

"Yes," said Max. "And I hope he has given that fellow a fright that will keep him from ever coming into these grounds again. If he isn't a scoundrel, his looks certainly belie him very much."

They held their ponies in check while watching the race between man and dog, but now urged them forward in haste to reach the house, for the short winter day was fast closing in.

The captain was standing on the veranda as they rode up.

"You are a trifle late, children," he said as he stepped to the side of Fairy and lifted Lulu from the saddle, but his tone was not stern.

"Yes, papa," said Max. "I'm afraid we went a little further than we ought. At any rate, it took us longer than we expected to reach home again. We were detained a minute or two just now, out there in the grove, by a tramp that caught hold of Fairy's bridle and wouldn't let go till I called Prince, and he showed his teeth."

"What! Can it be possible?" cried the captain, closing his fingers more firmly over the hand Lulu had slipped into his and gazing down into her face with a look of mingled concern and relief. "It is well indeed that Lulu was not alone, and that Prince was at hand. Come into the library and tell me all about it."

He led Lulu in as he spoke, Max following, while a servant took the horse and pony to their stable.

Captain Raymond sat down and drew Lulu to his side, putting his arm protectively around her, while Max, standing near, went on to give the particulars of their encounter with the tramp. Lulu now and then put in a word.

"Now, daughter," the captain said at the conclusion of the story. "I hope you are quite convinced of the wisdom and kindness of your father's prohibition of solitary rides and walks for you?"

"Yes, papa, I am, and I do not intend ever to disobey you again by taking them. I wasn't much frightened, but I know it would have been very dangerous for me if I'd been alone."

"No doubt of it," he said, caressing her with grave tenderness. "It almost makes me shudder to think of what might have happened had you been without a protector."

"And I doubt if I could have protected her without Prince's help, papa," said Max. "I think he's a valuable fellow and pays for his keep."

"Yes, I am glad I selected him as a Christmas gift for you," said his father. "But now I must warn you both to say nothing to or before Gracie about this occurrence, for timid as she is, it would be apt to cause her much suffering from apprehension."

"We will try to keep it a secret from her, papa," replied both children.

"In order to succeed in that you will have to be on your guard and give no hint of the matter in the presence of any of the servants."

"We will try to remember, papa," they promised with evident intention to do so.

"That is right," he said. "I think I can trust you not to forget or disobey. I know you would be loath to have your little sister tortured with nervous terrors. Now go and get yourselves ready for tea."

Lulu was full of excitement over her adventure, and through the evening found it difficult to refrain from speaking of it before Gracie. But, equally desirous to obey her father and to save her little sister from needless suffering, she resolutely put a curb upon her tongue till she found herself alone with him at bedtime.

Then she felt needful to go over the whole scene again. Seeing that it was a relief to her excitement, he let her run on about it to her heart's content.

"Has it made you feel at all timid tonight, daughter?" he asked kindly.

"No, papa," she answered promptly. "I don't think the man could get into the house, do you?"

"I think it most probable he has walked on till he is miles away from here by this time," the captain answered. "But even did we know him to be prowling around outside, we might rest and sleep in peace and security, assured that nothing can harm us without the will of our heavenly Father who loves us more than any earthly parent loves his child."

He drew her very close to his heart and imprinted a tender kiss upon her lips as he spoke.

"Yes, papa, it makes me feel very safe to remember that, thinking how dearly you love me. I know you would never let anything harm me if you could help it," she returned, putting an arm round his neck and hugging him tight. "Oh, I am glad that the Bible tells us that about God's love to us!"

"So am I, and that my children have early learned to love and trust Him.

"'Godliness is profitable unto all things, having promise of the life that now is, and of that which is to come.' That is not a promise that God's faithful followers shall be rich in this world's goods, but faith in God's loving care makes life happy even in the midst of poverty and pain. Riches have not the power to make us happy, but the love of God has.

"And those who begin to serve God in the morning of life and press onward and upward all their days, keeping near to Jesus and growing more and more like Him, will be happier in heaven—because of their greater capacity for the enjoyment of God and holiness—than the saved ones who sought him late in life or were less earnest in their endeavors to live in constant communication with Him and to bear more and more resemblance to Him.

"The Bible speaks of some who are 'scarcely saved,' and of others to whom 'an entrance shall be ministered abundantly into the everlasting kingdom of our Lord and Saviour Jesus Christ.'"

"Papa," said Lulu earnestly, "I want to be one of those. I want to live near to Jesus and grow every day more like Him. Oh, I am so little like Him now. Sometimes I fear not at all. Won't you help me all you can?"

"I will, my darling," he replied, speaking with emotion. "Every day I ask wisdom from on high for that very work—the work of helping you and all my dear children to be earnest, faithful servants of God."

The talk with her father had done much to quiet Lulu's excitement, and she fell asleep very soon after laying her head on her pillow.

It was still night when she awoke suddenly with the feeling that something unusual was going on in the house.

She sat up in bed and listened. She thought she heard a faint sound coming from the room below, and slipping from the bed she stole softly across the floor to the chimney, where there was a hot air flue beside the open fireplace.

Dropping down on her hands and knees, she put her ear close to the register and listened again, almost holding her breath in the effort to hear.

The chimney ran up between her bedroom and the little tower room opening into it. The library was under her bedroom and opening from it was the ground floor room of the tower, which was very strongly built. It had only the one door and very narrow slits of windows set high up in the thick stone walls.

In a safe in that small room were kept the family plate, jewelry, and money—though no very great amount of the last named, as the captain considered it far wiser to deposit it in the nearest bank.

The door of the strong room, as it was called, was of thick oak plank crossed with iron bars, and it had a ponderous bolt and a stout lock whose key was carried upstairs every night by the captain.

Listening with bated breath, Lulu's ear presently caught again the faint sound as of a file moving cautiously to and fro on metal.

"Burglars! I do believe it's burglars trying to steal the money and silver and Mamma Vi's jewelry that are in the safe," she said to herself with a thrill of mingled fear and excitement.

With that she crept into the tower room, softly opened the register there and applied her ear to it. The sound of the file seemed a trifle louder and presently she was sure she heard gruff voices, though she could not distinguish the words.

Her first impulse was to hurry to her father and tell him of her discovery. Her second thought was "If I do, papa will go down there, and maybe they'll kill him. And that would be a great, great deal worse than if they should carry off everything in the house. I wish I could catch them myself and lock them in there before I wake papa. Why couldn't I?" she thought, starting to her feet in extreme excitement.

"They're in the strong room, the bolt's on the library side, and probably they've left the key there, too, in the lock. If I'm going to try to do it, the sooner the better. I'll ask God to show me how and help me."

She knelt on the carpet for a moment, sending up her petition in a few earnest words, then rising, she stood for an instant, thinking very fast.

She could gain the library by a door opening into a back hall and very near the door into the strong room, whose door, if open, would be in a position to conceal her approach from the burglars till she could step behind it, so her scheme seemed not at all impracticable.

She hastily put on a dark dressing gown over her white night dress and thick felt slippers on her feet.

Her heart beat very fast as the thought occurred to her that there might be an accomplice in the library or hall, or that the door from the one into the other might creak and bring the miscreants rushing upon her before she could accomplish the task to which she had set herself.

"Well, what if they should, Lulu Raymond?" she asked, shutting her teeth hard together. "It 'twouldn't be half so bad as if they should harm your father. You could be very well spared, but he couldn't. Mamma Vi, Max, and Gracie would break their hearts if anything dreadful happened to him, and so would you, too. I'll try, trusting God to take care of me."

With swift, noiseless steps she passed out of her room, down a back stairway into the hall just spoken of, and gained the library door, finding it, to her great joy, wide enough open for her to slip in without even touching it.

She could see nothing there. The room was quite dark, but the sounds she heard were still going in the strong room, seeming a little louder now. The men must be in there at work on the safe with the door ajar, for a streak of light at the back between it and the jamb, told her it was not quite shut.

She crept to it and, peeping in at that crack, saw a man down on his knees working at the lock of the safe. Another stood close beside him, holding a dark lantern, open, so that the rays of light fell full and strongly upon the lock his confederate was trying to break.

Lulu could not see the face of the latter, his back being toward her, but as the other bent forward for a moment to watch the progress of the work, the light fell on his face, and she instantly recognized him as the tramp who had seized Fairy's bridle in the wood.

Trembling like a leaf she put up her hand and cautiously felt for the bolt. Holding tight to it and exerting all her strength, she suddenly slammed the door to and shot the bolt into its socket.

She heard the villains drop their tools, spring forward, and try the door with muttered oaths and curses. She waited to feel for the key and turn it in the lock, even to pull it out, and thrust it into the pocket of her gown. She did this last as a swift thought came to her that there might still be an accomplice lurking about who would release them if she left it there.

Then she ran as fast as her feet could carry her, through the library and hall, up the stairs, and on through the rooms, never stopping until she stood panting for breath beside her sleeping father.

She could not speak for a moment but laid her face on the pillow beside his and put her arm round his neck.

The touch roused him, and he asked, "Who is it? You, Lulu?"

"Yes, papa," she panted. "I—I've locked some burglars into the strong room and—"

"You? You have locked them in there?" he exclaimed in astonishment, starting up and drawing her into his arms. "Surely, my child, you have been dreaming."

"No, papa, not a bit. I've locked them in there and here's the key," putting it into his hand. "I slammed the door to on them. I shot the bolt, too, and I don't think they can get out. But what will we do? Papa, can you get somebody to help you take them to jail so you are not in danger all by yourself?"

"Yes, I shall telephone at once to the sheriff at Union, Lulu."

"Who is it? What ever is the matter?" asked Violet, as she awakened.

"I cannot wait at this moment to explain matters, my love," the captain said hastily, picking up Lulu and putting her in the place in the bed that he had just vacated. "I must act, leaving Lulu to tell her wild story."

With the last word, he hurried from the room, and the next moment they heard the telephone bell.

CHAPTER FIFTEENTH

"WHAT IS IT, LU?" Violet asked in trepidation. "Oh, what is the meaning of those awful sounds coming from below? Are burglars trying to break in?"

"No, Mamma Vi," returned Lulu with a little nervous laugh. "They are trying to break out."

"Break out? What can you mean, child?"

"They are locked into the strong room, Mamma Vi, and papa is calling for help to take them to jail. Hark! Don't you hear him?"

They sat up in the bed, listening intently.

"Hello!" the captain called. Then in another moment, "Captain Raymond of Woodburn wants the sheriff," they heard him say. "Ah, are you there. Mr. Wright? Burglars in the house. Burglars here. We have them fast, locked into the room with the safe they were trying to break open. Can you send a constable and several men to help him as promptly as you can?"

The reply was, of course, inaudible to the listeners in the bedroom, but the next moment the captain spoke again.

"Yes, I can hold them till you can get here, unless some outside accomplice should come to their aid."

He seemed to listen to a response, then a tinkle of the bell told that the conversation was at an end.

He turned at once to a private telephone connecting the dwelling with the outside cabins in which his menservants lodged and called them to come to his assistance.

Then back he went to his bedroom to reassure Violet and send Lulu to Gracie, who had awakened and was calling in affright to know what ever was the matter.

"Do not be alarmed, my dear," he said, as he hastily threw on his clothes. "I really think there is no cause for apprehension. But I must hurry down to admit the servants—I do not know if the burglars have left a door open or not—see in what condition things are in the lower rooms, and keep guard over my prisoners till the sheriff or constable and his men arrive."

"What can I do?" asked Violet.

"Stay here out of harm's way and be at the ready to soothe and quiet the children should they wake in affright," he answered, as he again hastened away.

Violet sprang from the bed and went with swift, noiseless steps into the nursery. All was quiet there, children and nurses soundly sleeping. She retraced her steps and went on into Gracie's room, where the two little girls were lying together in the bed, locked in each other's arms. Gracie was trembling with fear, and Lulu was bravely struggling with her own excitement, trying to calm and soothe her little sister.

"Oh, Mamma Vi, I'm glad you've come!" she exclaimed as Violet drew near. She then seated herself on the side of the bed and bent down to kiss first the one and then the other. "Gracie is so frightened."

"I'm so afraid those wicked men will hurt papa," sobbed Gracie.

"God will take care of him, dear child," Violet said, repeating her caress. "Besides, your papa just told me he thought there was no cause whatever for any apprehension.

"But, Lulu, I have not heard yet how the burglars came to be locked into the strong room. Tell me about it."

"Something awakened me, Mamma Vi, and I heard them. By listening a little, I made sure where they were. At first I thought I'd run and call papa, but then I thought there are two of them if not more and papa is only one. So he would hardly have a chance in trying to fight them. But if I should slip quietly down and slam the door to and lock them in, it would save risking papa's life. And if they should catch me and kill me, it wouldn't be half so bad as if they hurt papa.

"So I asked God to help me and take care of me. Then I ran down the back stairs to the library.

"The door into the back hall was far enough open to let me slip in without touching it. So that I did without making any noise to attract their attention. Then, seeing by the light coming from the crack at the back of the strong room door that they were in there, I crept close up, peeped in, and there they were—one down on his knees working at the lock of the safe, the other holding a lantern to give him light.

"When I had watched them for a minute, I asked God again to help me. Then I felt for the bolt and kept my hand on it while I, all of a sudden, pushed against the door with all my might, slammed it to, and shot the bolt in.

"I'd hardly done it when I heard the men drop their tools and run to the door to try to get it open.

They were saying the most dreadful words, too, that frightened me. So I only waited to lock the door with the key before I started to run upstairs and on through the rooms till I got to papa.

"He was asleep. I was so out of breath, and my heart was beating so fast I couldn't speak for a minute. But I put my arm round his neck and my cheek on the pillow close to his, and he woke."

"And it was you who locked the burglars in?" exclaimed Violet in astonishment. "I've heard before now of women doing such things but never of a little girl like you attempting it. You dear, brave, unselfish child! I am very, very proud of you!" and she bent down again and kissed Lulu several times.

The burglars, quite aware that their presence in the house was known, were making desperate efforts to escape, trying to force the lock or break down the door. At the same time, they were cursing and swearing in tones of concentrated fury.

The captain drew near and spoke to them.

"Men," he said sternly, "you are caught in a trap you have laid for yourselves, and escape is impossible. Both lock and door are strong enough to resist your utmost efforts. Therefore, you may as well take matters quietly."

"That we won't. Let us out, or it'll be worse for you!" growled on of the villains, grinding his teeth with rage.

"Have a little patience," returned the captain. "You shall be taken out presently and off the premises. You are by no means desirable inmates in the home of any honest, law-abiding citizen."

The response to that was a threat of vengeance to be taken later, should he dare deliver them to justice.

Finding their threats disregarded, they tried persuasion and appeals to his compassion—asserting that it was their first attempt to rob, and that they were driven to it by necessity. They told him how they and their families were in sore straits from extreme poverty, and they made grand promises to lead honest lives in the future.

One voice the captain recognized as that of the groom he had dismissed some months before because of his cruelty to Thunderer.

"Ajax," he said sternly, "you are lying to me! I know that your family are not in distress, and that you can make an honest living if you choose to be industrious and faithful to your employers. You were well paid here but lost your situation by inexcusable cruelty to dumb animals.

"Since discharging you, I have more than once supplied the wants of your wife and children. This is your grateful return, coming to rob me and bringing with you another, perhaps more desperate, villain than yourself."

The menservants had followed their master into the library and stood listening to the colloquy in open-mouthed astonishment.

"How dey git locked up in dar, cap'n?" asked one.

"Miss Lulu slammed the door on them and locked and bolted it," he replied, his eyes shining at the thought of the unselfish bravery of his child.

"Ki, cap'n! You's jokin', fo' shuah, dat little Miss Lu locked up de bugglars? How she gwine do dat? She one small chile an' dey two big men."

"She undoubtedly did it," returned the captain, smiling at the man's evident amazement. "She heard them at work with their tools on the safe door, came softly down into this room, peeped at them through the crack behind the door there, and before they were aware of her vicinity, slammed it to and bolted and locked it on them."

"Hurrah for little Miss Lu!" cried the men. Another one of them added, "Dey mus' hab her fo' a kunnel in de nex wah."

"No, sah, higher'n dat—fo' brigandine gineral at de berry leas'!" said another.

Seeing no hope of escape, the prisoners had ceased their efforts and awaited their certain fate in sullen silence.

They did not know who had been their captor, and in telling the story of Lulu's exploit, the captain purposely so lowered his tones that scarce a word reached their ears.

At this moment Max appeared at the door opening from the library into the front hall. He was only half dressed and was asking in much excitement what was the matter and what was the meaning of the lights and the noises that had awakened him.

His father explained in a few words, and as he finished, a loud knocking at the front entrance told of the arrival of the sheriff and his posse.

They were promptly admitted, filed into the library, and formed a semicircle about the door of the strong room—each man with a revolver in his hand, cocked and ready for instant use.

The door was then unfastened, and the burglars stepped out only to be immediately handcuffed and carried away to prison, sullenly submitting to their arrest because they saw that resistance was useless.

Before being taken from the house they were searched, and the captain's watch found upon Ajax. He had evidently visited the dressing room of his late master to obtain the key to the strong room door, and he had appropriated the watch at the same time.

The lock of the safe was examined and found but little injured. The scoundrels had not succeeded in getting at the valuables there.

They had collected together some from other parts of the house and made them into bundles ready to carry away, but they were uninjured and had only to be restored to their places.

Max was greatly excited. "Papa," he said when the sheriff had departed with his prisoners and the doors and windows were again secured, "we have had a narrow escape from serious loss, perhaps worse than that, for who knows but those fellows meant to murder us in our beds."

"I presume not, my son," replied the captain. "I think their only object was plunder, and that if they had succeeded in rifling the safe without discovery, they would have gone quietly away with their booty.

"Had they desired to kill any of us, they would have been likely to attempt it when upstairs in search of the key to the strong room."

"And it was Lu who spoiled their plans? Just think of it! I'd like to have had her chance. Papa, I think Lu's splendid!"

"She has certainly shown herself very brave and unselfish on this and several other occasions," the captain said with a happy look in his eyes.

"But come, we will do well now to go back to our beds, for it is scarcely four o'clock," he added, consulting his recovered watch.

The men servants had returned to their quarters, and father and son were alone.

Violet, in her dressing gown and slippers, met them at the head of the stairway.

"You have not been able to sleep, my love?" the captain said with a glance of concern at her pale, excited face. "But, of course, that could not be expected."

"No, we have been too much excited to close an eye," she answered. "They are gone? Do tell me about it!"

"Oh, papa, please come in here and tell it where Gracie and I can hear," called Lulu entreatingly from the inner room and the bed where they still lay clasped in each other's arms.

"I will. I think you deserve the indulgence," he said, going to them, Violet and Max following. The latter asked, "May I come in, too, papa?"

"Yes," replied his father, placing a chair for Violet. "I presume it will be a relief to you all to talk the matter over together with your mamma and me and perhaps you will be more inclined for sleep afterward."

"Papa, won't you sit down and take me on your knee and hug me close while you tell it?" entreated little Gracie.

"I will," he said, doing as she requested. Then catching a longing look in Lulu's eyes, he said, "You may come, too, daughter. Slip on your dressing gown and stand here by my side. I have an arm for you as well as one for Gracie."

Lulu promptly and joyfully availed herself of his permission.

"Lu," said Max, "you're a real heroine! Brave as a lion! I'm proud to own you for my sister. I'm afraid I mightn't have been half so brave."

"Oh, yes, Max, I'm sure you would have done just the same," she returned, blushing with pleasure. "But you see I preferred to do it, because I thought they might kill papa, and that would have been, oh, so much worse than being killed myself!" clinging lovingly to her father and hiding her face on his shoulder as she spoke.

"Dear child!" he said in moved tones, clasping her close. "You have a very strong and unselfish love for me."

"Papa, it would have broken my heart, and Mamma Vi's, and Max's, and Gracie's, too, if anything dreadful had happened to you."

"And what about papa's heart if he should lose his dear little daughter Lulu, or if anything dreadful should happen to her?"

"I didn't have time to think about that, papa. I know you love me very much and would be sorry to lose me—naughty as I often am—but you have other children, and I have only one father. So, of course, it would be a great deal worse for me to lose you and all the rest to lose you, too."

"The worst thing that could befall us," said Violet. "But, Lulu, dear, we all love you and would feel it a terrible thing to have you killed or badly injured in any way."

"Indeed, we would!" exclaimed Max with a slight tremble in his voice.

"Oh, I couldn't ever, ever bear it!" sobbed Gracie, throwing an arm round her sister's neck.

"Well," said the captain cheerfully, hugging both at once, "we have escaped all the evils we have been talking of. Our heavenly Father has taken care of us, and we have not even lost our worldly goods, much less our lives. We may well trust Him for the future and not fear what men can do unto us."

"Yes," said Violet. "We know that He has all power in heaven and earth, and that He will never suffer any real evil to befall one of His people. 'He will not suffer thy foot to be moved; He that keepeth thee will not slumber.'

"Levis, did you know those men?"

"One of them is Ajax."

"Is it possible?" she exclaimed. "What a return for all the kindness you have shown to him and his!"

"Ajax? There, I was sure I heard Ajax's voice in the hall while the sheriff was here," cried Lulu. "He must have been the one who was down on his knees trying to break the safe lock when I peeped in at the crack. I didn't see his face. But the other was a white man."

"Yes," said Max, "a man we'd seen before."

"The tramp you saw?" asked his father.

"Yes, sir."

"I recognized him, too," said Lulu. "Papa, what will be done with him and Ajax?"

"They will have to be tried for burglary and if convicted, will be sent to the penitentiary for a term of years."

"Papa, will we have to appear as witnesses on the trial?" asked Max.

"Yes."

"The men did not attempt any resistance to the arrest?" Violet said inquiringly.

"No, they saw it would be quite useless."

After a little more talk the captain said, "Now, I think it will be best for us all to go to our beds again and try to sleep till the usual hour for rising."

"Papa, I feel so afraid," said Gracie, holding tight to him as he tried to put her in the bed.

"My darling, try not to feel so," he said, caressing her. "Try to believe that God will take care of you."

"Please ask Him again, papa," she pleaded.

Then they all knelt while the captain asked in a few simple words that He who neither slumbers nor sleeps would be their shield, defending them from all evil, and that trusting in His protecting care, they might be able to banish every fear and lay down in peace and sleep.

"I am not afraid now, papa," Gracie said, as they rose from their knees. "You may please put me in bed, and I think I'll go to sleep directly, for I'm very tired."

"You will allow them to sleep past the usual hour, my dear, will you not?" asked Violet.

"Yes," he said. "I wish you children to sleep on as long as you can, and if possible make up all you have lost by the visit of the burglars. It will not matter if you take your breakfast later than usual by even so much as an hour or two."

"But that will make us late for lessons, papa," suggested Max.

"Which I will excuse for once," returned his father with an indulgent smile.

CHAPTER SIXTEENTH

DAY HAD FULLY DAWNED before the Woodburn household was astir, and it was long past his accustomed hour when the captain paid his usual morning visit to his little daughters.

He found them up and dressed and ready with a glad greeting. "Were you able to sleep, my darlings?" he asked, caressing them in turn.

"Oh, yes, indeed, papa. We slept nicely," the two both answered.

"And do you feel refreshed and well this morning?"

"Yes, papa, thank you very much for letting us sleep so long."

"I allowed myself the same privilege," he said pleasantly. "We will have no school today. I have already been notified that there will be a preliminary examination of the prisoners before the magistrate this morning, and that Lulu, Max, and I must attend as witnesses."

"I'd rather not go, papa. Please, don't make me," pleaded Lulu.

"My child, it is not I, but the law, that insists," he said. "But you need not feel disturbed over the matter. You have only to tell a straightforward story of what you heard and saw and did in connection with the attempted robbery.

"I am very thankful," he went on, "that I have always found my little daughter perfectly truthful."

"Max, too, papa?"

"Yes, Max, too. And when you give your testimony, I want you to remember that God—the God of truth, who abhors deceit and the deceitful and who knows all things—hears every word you say."

Taking up Lulu's Bible and opening it at the twenty-fourth psalm, he read, "He that hath clean hands and a pure heart; who hath not lifted up his soul unto vanity, nor sworn deceitfully, he shall receive the blessing from the Lord, and righteousness from the God of his salvation."

Then turning to the twenty-first chapter of Revelation, "All liars shall have their part in the lake which burneth with fire and brimstone."

Closing the Book and laying it aside, "My dear children," he said earnestly and with grave tenderness, "you see how God hates lying and deceit, how sorely He will punish them if not repented of and forsaken. Speak the truth always though at the risk of torture and death. Never tell a lie though it should be no more than to assert that two and two do not make four.

"Be courteous to all so far as you can without deceit, but never, never allow your desire to be polite to betray you into words or acts that are not strictly truthful."

The children were evidently giving very earnest heed to their father's words.

"Papa," said Gracie, sighing and hiding her blushing face on his shoulder, "you know I did once say what was not true, but I'm very, very sorry. I've asked God many times to forgive me for Jesus' sake, and I believe He has."

"I've no doubt of it, my darling," returned her father. "For, 'if we confess our sins, He is faithful and just to forgive us our sins, and to cleanse us from all unrighteousness.'"

"I don't believe Lu ever did," said Gracie. "She's a great deal better girl than I am."

"No, it is not that I am better than you," was Lulu's emphatic dissent from that. "It's only that I am not timid like you. If I had been, it's very likely I'd have told many an untruth to hide my faults and keep from being punished."

"The telephone bell is ringing, papa," announced Max, looking in at the door.

The call was from Ion. A vague report of last night's doings at Woodburn had just reached the family there, and they were anxious to learn the exact truth.

The captain gave the facts briefly and suggested that some of the Ion friends drive over and hear them in detail.

It was replied that several of them would do so shortly, Grandma Elsie being among them, and that she would spend the day, keeping Violet company during her husband's absence at Union, if, as she supposed, Vi's preference should be for remaining at home.

"Of course it will," said Violet, who was standing near. "Please tell mamma I'll be delighted to have her company."

The captain delivered the message, and all hurried down to breakfast.

"Everything is in it's usual order, I see, Levis," Violet remarked, glancing about the hall and in at the library door as they passed it. "Really, it seems to me that the terrible events of last night seem more like an unpleasant dream than of actual occurrences."

"Christine has been up for several hours and busied in having everything set to rights," the captain said in reply.

As usual, family worship followed directly upon breakfast, and it was scarcely over when the Ion carriage drove up with Grandma Elsie, Harold, and Herbert accompanying it on horseback.

"Captain, I am greatly interested in this affair," said Harold, shaking hands with his brother-in-law. "Indeed, we all are for that matter, and Herbert and I propose going over to Union to be present at the examination of the prisoners.

"Is your strong room on exhibition? I own to a feeling of curiosity in regard to it."

"You are privileged to examine it at any time," returned Captain Raymond with a good-humored laugh. "I will take you there at once if you wish, for we will have to be setting off on our ride presently.

"Mother, would you like to see it also?"

"Yes, and to hear the story of the capture while looking in upon its scene."

The captain led the way, all the rest following, except Lulu, who stole quietly away to her room to get herself ready for the trip to town.

She shrank a little from the thought of facing the two desperados and testifying against them, but she kept up her courage by thinking that both her heavenly Father and her earthly one would be with her to protect and help her. She was encouraged also by remembrance of her papa's assurance that she need not feel disturbed. All she had to do was to tell a plain, straightforward story — "the truth, the whole truth, and nothing but the truth."

"I can do that," she said to herself. "It will be quite easy, for I remember perfectly all about it.

Those wicked men threatened papa that if he had them sent to jail they'd kill him some day when they are let out again. I suppose they'll want to kill me, too, for telling about it in court, but I know they can't do us any harm while God takes care of us. That must be the meaning of that verse in Proverbs I learned the other day.

"'There is no wisdom nor understanding nor counsel against the Lord.'

"And the next verse says, 'safety is of the Lord.' So I'm sure we needn't be afraid of them."

Captain Raymond opened the door of the strong room and called attention to the marks of the burglars' tools on the lock of the safe.

"It was Lulu who first became aware of their presence in the house," he said. "And she—why, where is the child?" as he turned to look for her and perceived that she had disappeared.

"I think she has gone upstairs to put on her hat and coat," Violet said.

"Ah, yes, I suppose so! Leaving me to tell the story of her bravery and presence of mind myself."

He proceeded to do so and was well-satisfied with the encomiums upon his child which it called forth from Grandma Elsie and her sons.

"I congratulate you, captain, upon being the father of a little girl who can show such unselfish courage," Grandma Elsie said with enthusiasm, her eyes shining with pleasure. "I am proud of her myself, the dear, brave child!"

"And so am I," said Violet. "But of course," with a mischievous laughing glance into her husband's face, "her father is not but considers her a very ordinary specimen of childhood. Is not that so, my dear?"

"Ah, my love, don't question me too closely," he returned with a smile in his eyes that said more plainly than words that he was a proud, fond father to the child whose conduct was under discussion.

But at that moment the carriage was announced. Lulu came running down ready for her trip, her father handed her in, and then seated himself and put his arm around her, looking down into her face with a tenderly affectionate smile.

"You will not find it a very severe ordeal, my daughter," he said.

"You're not afraid, Lu, are you?" asked Max.

"No, not with papa close by to take care of me and tell me what to do," she answered, nestling closer to her father.

"No," said Max. "And the burglars wouldn't be allowed to hurt you anyhow. The magistrate and the sheriff and the rest would take care of that, you know."

"I suppose so," returned Lulu. "But for all that, it would be dreadful to have to go there without papa. You wouldn't want to yourself, Max?"

"I'd a great deal rather have papa along, of course. Anybody would want his intimate friend with him on such an occasion, and papa is my most intimate friend," replied the lad with a laughing but most affectionate look into his father's face.

"That's right, my boy. I trust you will always let me be that to you," the captain said, grasping his son's hand and holding it for a moment in a warm, affectionate clasp.

"You are mine, too, papa, my best and dearest earthly friend," Lulu said, lifting eyes shining with filial love to his. "Papa, aren't you afraid those bad men will try to harm you some day, if they ever get out of prison?"

"We are always safe in the path of duty," he replied. "And it is a duty we owe the community to bring such lawless men to justice for the protection of those they would prey upon. No, I do not fear them, because I am under the protection of Him 'in whose hand is the soul of every living thing, and the breath of all mankind.'

"'The Lord is my light and my salvation; whom shall I fear? The Lord is the strength of my life; of whom shall I be afraid?'

"No, daughter, one who fears God need fear nothing else—neither men nor devils—for our God is stronger than Satan and all his hosts."

"Wicked men are Satan's servants, aren't they?"

"Yes, for they do his will, obey his behests."

"It seems to me Christians ought to be very happy, always," remarked Max.

"Yes, they ought," said his father. "The command is, 'Rejoice in the Lord always,' and it is only a lack of faith that prevents any of us from doing so."

Arrived at their destination, they found a little crowd of idlers gathered about the door of the magistrate's office whither the two prisoners had been taken a few moments before. As the Woodburn carriage drove up and the captain and his children alighted from it, the crowd parted to let them pass in, several of the men lifting their hats with a respectful, "Good morning, sir," to the captain. "Good morning, Master Max."

Their salutations were politely returned, and the captain stepped into the office, holding Lulu by the hand, who was closely followed by Max.

Harold and Herbert had arrived a little in advance and were among the spectators who, with the officers and their prisoners, nearly filled the small room.

The children behaved very well indeed, showing by their manner when taking the oath to tell "the truth, the whole truth, and nothing but the truth," that they were duly impressed with the solemnity of the act and the responsibility they were assuming.

Lulu was, of course, the principal witness. Her modest, self-possessed bearing, equally free from boldness and forwardness on the one hand and bashfulness and timidity on the other, pleased her father extremely. She won the admiration of all present, as did her simple, straightforward way of telling her story.

The evidence was so full that the magistrate had no hesitation in committing the accused for trial at the approaching spring term of court. In default of bail, they were sent back to prison.

❧ ❧ ❧ ❧ ❧

"Take me to the nursery, Vi," Grandma Elsie said, when the departure of the party destined for the magistrate's office had left them alone together. "I feel that an hour with my grandchildren will be quite refreshing. The darlings are scarcely less dear to me than were their mother and her brothers and sisters in their infancy."

"And they are so fond of you, mamma," responded Violet, leading the way.

Little Elsie sent up a glad shout at the sight of her grandmother. "I so glad, I so glad! P'ease take Elsie on your lap, g'amma, and tell pitty 'tories."

"Oh, don't begin teasing for stories the very first minute," said Violet. "You'll tire poor grandma."

"No, mamma, Elsie won't tease, 'cause papa says it's naughty. But dear g'amma likes to tell Elsie 'tories, don't you, g'amma?" climbing into her grandmother's lap.

"Yes, dear, grandma enjoys making her little girl happy," Mrs. Travilla replied, fondly caressing the little prattler. "What story shall it be this time?"

"'Bout Adam and Eve eatin' dat dapple."

Grandma kindly complied, telling the old story of the fall in simple language suited to the infant comprehension of the baby girl, who listened with as deep an interest as though it were a new tale to her, instead of an oft-repeated one.

On its conclusion, she sat for a moment as if in profound thought, then looking up into her grandmother's face, she asked, "Where is dey now?"

"In heaven, I trust."

"Elsie's goin' to ask dem 'bout dat when Elsie gets to heaven."

"About what, darling?"

"'Bout eatin' dat apple—what dey do it for."

"It was very wicked for them to take it, because God had forbidden them to do so."

"Yes, g'amma, Elsie wouldn't take apple if papa say no."

"No, I hope not. It is very naughty for children to disobey their papa or mamma. And we must all obey God our heavenly Father."

"G'amma, p'ease tell Elsie 'bout heaven."

"Yes, darling, I will. It is a beautiful place with streets of gold, a beautiful river, and trees with delicious fruits. It is never dark, for there is never night there. And Jesus our dear Saviour is there and is the light thereof, so that they do not need the sun or moon for light.

"Nobody is ever sick, sorry, hungry, or in pain. Nobody is ever naughty. They all love God and one another. There is very sweet music there. They wear white robes and have crowns of gold on their heads and golden harps in their hands."

"To make sweet music?"

"Yes."

"Dey wear white dess?"

"Yes."

"Do dey button up behind like Elsie's dess?"

Violet laughed at that question. "She is very desirous to have her dresses fasten in front like mamma's," she explained in reply to her mother's look of surprised inquiry.

"Do dey, g'amma? Do dey button up in de back?"

"I don't know how they are made, my little dearie," her grandma answered. "I never was there to see them."

"Elsie's never dere."

"No, people don't go there till they die."

"Elsie's never dere 'cept when Elsie's gettin' made. Wasn't Elsie dere den? Didn't Dod make Elsie up in heaven?"

"No, darling, you were never there, but if you love Jesus, He will take you there some day."

"Mamma, how nicely you answer or parry her questions," said Violet. "As her father says, 'She can ask some that a very wise man could not answer.'"

"Yes, she has an inquiring mind, and I would not discourage her desire to learn by asking questions," Grandma Elsie said. Then she added with a smile, "I can remember that her mother used to ask me some puzzling ones twenty years ago."

"And I never received a rebuff but was always answered to the best of your ability, dear mamma. I think of that now when tempted to impatience with my little girl's sometimes wearisome questioning, and I resolve to try to be as good a mother to her as you were to me—and still are," she added with a loving smile. "And now that she has gone back to her play and baby Ned is sleeping, I want a quiet chat with you."

"Then let us go to your boudoir and have it then," her mother answered, rising and moving toward the door.

"Mamma, I have not heretofore been timid about burglars," Violet said when they were seated in the boudoir, each busied with a bit of needlework. "But I fear that I shall be in the future. Only think, mamma, how near they were to my husband and myself while we lay sleeping soundly in our own room! How easily they might have murdered us both before we were even aware of their presence in the house."

"Could they? Had you then no wakeful guardian at hand?"

"Oh, mamma, yes! 'Lo, I am with you always, even unto the end of the world,' and 'He that keepeth Israel shall neither slumber nor sleep.' And yet—haven't even Christians sometimes been murdered by burglars?"

"I cannot assert that they have not," replied her mother. "'According to your faith be it unto you,' and even true Christians are sometimes lacking in faith—putting their trust in their own defenses, or some earthly helper, instead of the Keeper of Israel, or they are fearful and doubtful, refusing to take God at His word and rest in His protecting care.

"I do not see that we have anything to do with the question you propounded just now. We have only to take God's promises, believe them fully, and be without carefulness in regard to that, as well as other things. I am perfectly sure He will suffer no real evil to befall any who thus trust in Him.

"Death by violence may sometimes be a shorter, easier passage home than death from disease, and come in whatever shape it may, death can be no calamity to the Christian.

"Solomon tells us that the day of death is better than the day of one's birth. 'Blessed are the dead which die in the Lord.'

"My dear Vi, I think one who can claim all the promises of God to His children should be utterly free from the fear that hath torment—should be afraid of nothing whatever but that which is both displeasing and dishonoring to God."

"Yes, mamma, I see that it is so, and that all I lack to make me perfectly courageous and easy in mind is stronger faith.

"I think my husband has a faith that lifts him above every fear. He seems perfectly content to leave all future events to the ordering of his heavenly Father."

Grandma Elsie's eyes shone. "You are blest in having such a husband, my dear Vi," she said. "I trust you will help each other on in the heavenly way and be fellow-helpers to your children and his."

Violet looked up brightly. "I trust we shall, mamma. We both earnestly desire to be, and I think his three all give good evidence that they have already begun to walk in the straight and narrow way. It's no wonder, considering what a faithful, loving, Christian father he is — so constant in prayer and effort on their behalf."

"Ah," Grandma Elsie said, as the sound of wheels was heard on the driveway, "they have returned. Now we shall have a report of all that was done in the magistrate's office. It must have been quite an ordeal to both Max and Lulu."

CHAPTER
SEVENTEENTH

CAPTAIN RAYMOND WAS met at the door by the youngest two of his daughters.

"Papa, I'se been yaisin' seeds," announced little Elsie, running into his arms.

"Yaisin' seeds," he echoed. "What on earth can that mean?"

"She means seeding raisins, papa," explained Gracie with a merry laugh. "We've been in the kitchen helping the cook. At least pretending to help her. Perhaps we hindered more than we helped."

"I dare say," he responded. "But I hope Elsie didn't eat the raisins—nor you either. They are quite too indigestible for your young stomachs."

"We each had one, papa. That was all. I told Elsie we shouldn't eat any more till we asked leave, and she was a good girl and didn't tease for more."

"That was right, but for your own sakes I must say that is all you can have."

He had paused for a moment in the hall to hug and kiss the two. Max and Lulu stood looking on. Harold and Herbert were taking off their overcoats near by.

"You're a funny talker, Elsie," laughed Max.

"Your English is not of the purest, little woman," said her Uncle Harold.

"Tell Uncle Harold he must not expect perfection in a beginner," said her father. "Where are grandma and mamma?"

"In the parlor, I believe," said Gracie. "Oh, no! See, they are just coming downstairs."

"Yes, here we are," said Violet. "And both quite anxious for a report of the morning's proceedings in the magistrate's office. Won't you walk into the parlor, gentlemen and ladies, and let us have it?"

"Certainly, we will be very happy to gratify your very excusable curiosity," returned her husband laughingly, as she came to his side. He stooped his tall form to give her the kiss with which he never failed to greet her after even a brief separation.

The older people all repaired to the parlor, but the children did not follow.

"I must go and look over my lessons," said Max.

"And I'm going to my room," said Lulu. "Gracie, if you will come with me, I'll tell you all about the trial — if that's what you call it."

"Oh, yes, do!" responded Gracie, as the two started up the stairs together. "Were you scared, Lu?"

"No, I didn't feel frightened, for I'm not timid, you know, and papa was near me all the time. He'd told me all I had to do was to tell a straightforward, truthful story.

"I did hate to take the oath, but I knew I had to and that it wasn't wrong, though it does seem a dreadful thing to do."

"It isn't like other swearing," remarked Max, who was moving up the stairs somewhat ahead of his sisters. "There must be a right kind, because in the Psalms, where David is describing a good man, he says of him, 'He that sweareth to his own hurt and changeth not.'"

"Yes, I know," said Lulu. "I can see the difference. This must be the right kind or papa would never have let me do it."

"How do they do it?" asked Gracie. "How did you do it, Lu?"

"A man said over the words for me—a promise to 'tell the truth, the whole truth, and nothing but the truth'—and I promised by kissing the Bible. That was all."

"That wasn't very hard to do," said Gracie. "But, oh, I'd have been so frightened to have to tell something with so many people listening!"

"Of course, because you're such a weak, timid little thing. But I'm big and strong and not afraid of things like that.

"There were a good many people there. The room was quite full, but I felt that that did not make much difference when I thought about God hearing every word I said and knowing if it was really the truth, the whole truth, and nothing but the truth.

"Ajax's wife was there, crying fit to break her heart, too, 'specially when they took him back to jail.

"Papa stopped and spoke to her before we went into the carriage to come home. He said he was sorry for her. He said if she continued to be honest and industrious, he would see that she did not want. He hoped her husband would some day come out of prison a better man."

"Did she seem thankful to papa?" asked Gracie.

"Yes, and she said she didn't see how Ajax could be so bad and ungrateful as to try to steal papa's money after he'd been so kind to both her and to the children."

"Yes, and I pity 'Liza for being his wife, and the children because they have such a bad father."

"Lu, let's ask papa if we mayn't buy some calico and other things with some of our benevolence money and make clothes for them."

"I wouldn't mind giving the money," said Lulu. "But I hate to sew on such things. You know I never did like plain sewing. I'll see about it, though."

"You'd do it to please the dear Lord Jesus, even though you don't like it?" asked Gracie softly.

"Yes, that I will, if papa approves," returned Lulu warmly, her eyes shining. "Gracie, it's good—a real pleasure, I mean—to make yourself do distasteful things for Jesus' sake.

"I'll put my hat and coat in their proper places and smooth my hair, so I'll be neat for dinner, and we'll go talk to papa about it at once. He's sure to approve, and I don't want to give myself any chance to change my mind and give the thing up!"

"We won't mind Grandma Elsie hearing," added Gracie. "Perhaps she'll know what they need the most, and maybe she'll tell Rosie and Eva and they'll offer to do something for the poor things, too."

"Oh, yes, perhaps we can form ourselves into a Dorcas society. That's what they call societies that make garments for the poor, you know, because of Dorcas in the Bible who made coats and garments for the poor where she lived."

"Yes, Lu, but there's the dinner bell, and we'll have to wait awhile before we can talk to papa about it. You know he says we mustn't talk a great deal at the table when there's company."

"And I have to smooth my hair yet, and that will make me late. I'm so sorry because it vexes papa to have us unpunctual. Don't wait for me, Gracie, for that will make you late, too."

"I'd rather wait for you, but I s'pose I ought to go at once," Gracie said, looking regretfully back as she left the room.

The blessing had been asked, and the captain was carving the turkey when Lulu took her seat at the table, which was close at his right hand.

He gave her a grave look.

"I'm very sorry I'm late, papa," she said in a low tone, casting her eyes down. "I'd been so busy talking with Gracie that I hadn't had my hair smoothed when the bell rang."

"It has been a very exciting morning for you, daughter, and I'll excuse you this time," he returned, speaking kindly and in as low a key as her own. "It is not often I find you unpunctual."

Lulu heaved a sigh of relief, her countenance brightened, and her eyes were lifted to her father's face with a grateful, loving look that brought a smile to his lips and eyes.

She was very quiet during the meal, speaking only when spoken to, but her father kept an eye on her plate and saw that her wants and needs were abundantly supplied.

On leaving the table all repaired to the parlor and Lulu and Gracie, seizing the first opportunity offered them by a pause in the talk of their elders, told of their plan and asked permission to carry it out.

It was received with the entire approval by all present, their father included.

"I have no doubt that Rosie and Evelyn will be glad to join you in forming a Dorcas society," said Grandma Elsie. "If you'd like, I shall be happy to cut out garments for you to work upon and to teach you how to do it for yourself."

"Oh, thank you, ma'am!" responded the little girls. "We were sure you would and that would be ever so nice."

"Taridge tumin'! Two taridge tumin'!" cried little Elsie, who had climbed on a chair and was gazing out of a window looking upon the drive.

They proved to be the Ion and Fairview carriages, bringing the whole family of the latter place and all of the other who were not already present.

"We have come in a body, as you see, to learn all about the strange occurrences of last night and the consequent doings in the magistrate's office this morning," Grandpa Dinsmore remarked, as he shook hands with the captain and kissed Violet, first on one cheek, then on the other.

"Tiss Elsie, too, dampa," cried the little one toddling up to him. "Oo mustn't fordet to tiss oor 'ittle dirl."

"Certainly not," he said, taking her into his arms to kiss her several tines, then sitting down with her on his knee. "Do you know that you are my great-granddaughter, Elsie?"

"Ess, Elsie knows dat," she answered, nodding her curly head wisely.

Meantime greetings had been exchanged among the others, and the four little girls had already gotten into a corner by themselves.

"Oh, Lu, do tell us all about it!" cried Rosie. "I never did hear of such a brave girl as you! Why I'd have been scared to death and never have thought of such a thing as going down where the burglars were about."

"Oh, I think you would if you'd been in my place," returned Lulu modestly. "You see, I was afraid if I waited to tell papa about them, they might come out and see him ready to fight them and kill him. But I thought if I could get the door shut and fastened on them before they knew anybody was there, nobody would be hurt."

"And that's the way it was," said Evelyn. "But you were a brave girl, and there's no use in your denying it."

"Yes, indeed, you were," said Rosie. "But come now, do tell us the whole story. We want to hear it fresh from your lips."

"And what went on in the magistrate's office, too," added Eva. "Oh, didn't you dislike having to go there and testify?"

"Yes, I begged papa not to make me, but he said it was the law, and not he, that insisted."

"Yes, I know, and of course those things have to be done in such cases. But I hope my turn will never come. Now, Lu, please begin. You'll have at least two very attentive listeners."

"More than that, I think," said Rosie, as other voices were heard in the hall, quickly followed by the entrance of the relatives from the Oaks, the Pines, and Roselands.

Greetings were scarcely exchanged with these when the families from Ashlands and the Laurels joined the circle so that quite a large surprise party had gathered there unexpectedly to themselves as well as to their hosts. The same desire—to learn the full particulars of what had reached them as little more than a vague report—had brought them all.

These were given, and Lulu received so much commendation and was so lauded for her bravery that her father began to fear she would be puffed up with vanity and conceit.

But at length that subject was dropped and the one of the proposed Dorcas society taken up.

Evelyn seemed quietly pleased and interested, Zoe, Lora, and Rosie ready to enter into the work with enthusiasm, while the Dinsmore girls gave a rather languid attention to the discussion.

But when it had been decided to organize a society on the spot, and the business of electing officers was taken up, they roused themselves to a new interest. Maud was evidently gratified when Evelyn nominated her for the secretaryship.

Lulu seconded the motion, and Maud was unanimously elected.

Zoe had already been made president. Lora was chosen treasurer. These were all the officers considered necessary, but Sydney, Evelyn, and Lulu were appointed a committee to visit the poor families in the neighborhood and learn what articles of clothing were most needed by them.

It was decided that the society should meet once a fortnight at one or the other of the homes of the members, taking them in turn. It was also decided that at these meetings reports should be given as to the state of the finances, work done, and articles needed. Finished garments would also be brought in, examined, and pronounced upon as well- or ill-done. The members would busy themselves in cutting and basting new garments while together, and each carry home with her one or more to be made in the interval between that and the next meeting.

Also, each member was to consider herself under appointment to invite her young girl or young lady friends from other families to join with them in the good work.

"Now I think that is all," said Grandma Elsie. "You are fully organized, and I invite you to hold your first meeting at Ion next Wednesday afternoon. That will give time for ascertaining the needs of some of those we wish to assist and for the purchase of materials."

"But how are your funds to be raised, Elsie?" asked her father.

"By a tax on the members and contributions from their friends, which will be thankfully accepted," she said with a pleased smile as he took out his wallet and handed her a five dollar bill. "We are very much obliged, sir."

The captain and the other gentlemen present—some of the ladies also—immediately followed Mr. Dinsmore's example.

Then the question of the amount of tax on the members was discussed and settled.

After that the captain said he had a suggestion to make—namely, that it would be well for the little girls to be accompanied by an older person when making their visits to their proposed beneficiaries.

"It will require some wisdom and tact to make the necessary investigations without wounding the feelings of those they desire to benefit or injuring their commendable pride of independence," he said in conclusion.

"Thank you for the advice, captain," Grandma Elsie replied. "I think it most wise. What have the members of the society to say about it?"

All responded promptly that they would prefer to have an older person with them on those occasions.

"And we'd better begin that business tomorrow," said Zoe. "So that whoever is to do the buying of materials to be cut and basted at the first meeting may have the needed information in season."

"I hope Grandma Elsie will buy the things," said Lulu. "Don't you all vote for that, girls?"

"Yes, yes, indeed. If she will," they all answered, and all were pleased that she at once consented to do so.

"Are we boys to be shut out of all this?" asked Max. "I don't see why we shouldn't take hold of such work as well as the girls. I'm conceited enough to think I could wield a pair of shears and cut out garments by a pattern or under instruction. And I know I can run a sewing machine, for I've tried it."

"Certainly we could all help with the financial part," said Chester Dinsmore.

"Let's take them in," said Sydney. "We want all the money we can get."

"Of course we do," said Lora. "The more money we have the more good we may hope to do."

The others seemed to see the force of the argument and all voted unanimously for the admission of the lads.

"What about the home and foreign missionary societies?" asked Evelyn. "I thought we had decided to have one of each just among ourselves. Was it the girls only? Or will the boys take part in them, too?"

"Of course, we will, if you'll let us," replied Max. "And you can't have too much money for them, seeing there are millions upon millions of heathen to be taught and furnished with Bibles."

"Yes," said the captain, "boys should be as much interested in mission work as girls, and I see no reason why you young relatives and friends should not work together.

"But with your studies and other duties to attend to, children, you have hardly time for such a multiplication of societies. As the work is one, the field the world, I propose that you form only one more society, which shall be for both home and foreign missions."

"A very good plan, I think also," commented Grandpa Dinsmore.

"I propose that we proceed at once to organize such a society," said Zoe.

"And shouldn't we have gentlemen officers?" asked Lulu. "I think Uncle Harold would make a good president."

"Thank you," he said, smiling pleasantly on her. "But I could not serve because I must be off to college directly."

"And the same objection applies to all of us except Max and little Walter," added Chester Dinsmore. "We older lads can only pay our dues and perhaps meet with you occasionally when at home on a vacation."

"Working for the good cause in the meantime, in whatever place we are," added Harold.

"Should we proceed to organize?" asked Zoe.

"Yes, if Grandma Elsie will help us as she did with the Dorcas," said Lulu.

The others joined in the request, and Grandma Elsie kindly complied.

Eva was chosen president, Rosie treasurer, and they would have made Lulu secretary but that she strenuously declined, insisting that she wasn't ready enough with her pen to find time for that in addition to all the sewing and other things she was undertaking.

"Then I nominate Max," said Rosie, giving him a bright look and smile.

"And I second the motion," said Evelyn.

Max made no objection and seemed gratified when he was pronounced unanimously elected.

They then settled the amount of their yearly subscription to each cause and the time of meeting, deciding that it should be on the same day and hour as the meeting of the other society, but on the alternate week.

"What will we do at our meetings?" asked Sydney.

"What other people do at missionary meetings, I presume," answered Zoe. "Read the Bible, sing hymns, pray for the missionaries and the heathen at home and abroad."

"Pay in our dues, too," said Max. "And I suppose each one will try to find some interesting article to take to the meeting to be read aloud to the others."

"Yes, of course, we must do all that if we want to have very enjoyable meetings," said Zoe.

"And we older people must see to it that you are well supplied with literature bearing upon that subject," said the captain.

He was rejoiced to perceive that the interest of these new enterprises was taking his children's thoughts from the unpleasant occurrences of the previous night. Almost all their talk with him that evening when the guests had gone and the babies were being put to bed was of the work they hoped to do in connection with their missionary and Dorcas societies.

To Lulu had been assigned the duty of visiting the family of Ajax for the purpose of learning what were their most pressing needs in the line of clothing.

Speaking of it, she asked, "Ought I not to go tomorrow, papa? And will you go with me?"

"I say yes to both questions," he replied. "You may be ready for your call directly when we are finished with school duties. That will give us time to go and return in good season for dinner."

"Yes, sir, I'll be ready. Thank you very much for promising to take me."

"'Liza must feel lonesome tonight, thinking about Ajax in jail," remarked Gracie thoughtfully. "But I'm glad he's there so that he can't be trying to break into anybody's house. Papa, could he get out and come here again?"

"It is hardly possible," answered her father, looking tenderly down into her face and smoothing her curls with a caressing hand. "And he would not want to hurt you if he could come into the house. I don't see how anyone could wish to harm my gentle, kindhearted, little Gracie."

"Papa, shall I sleep in her bed with her tonight?" asked Lulu.

"Certainly, if she would like it."

"Oh, I should!" Gracie exclaimed. "I know our heavenly Father will take care of me, but it's good to feel Lu's arm around me, too."

"Then you shall," said Lulu, giving her a very affectionate pat. "Your big sister likes to take good care of you."

CHAPTER
EIGHTEENTH

"OH, LU, TELL ME about it!" exclaimed Gracie when Lulu came home the next day from her visit to Eliza. "Are they very poor and needy?"

"'Liza and her children? Well, not so very, because papa has been seeing to them for quite awhile. They had a good fire—'Liza has been ironing for somebody—and pretty good clothes, but the children are growing too big for some of their things and have torn or worn holes in others. So papa says he thinks we should make them some new ones. I'm going to ask Grandma Elsie to buy some flannel with some of my money and let me make a shirt for the baby."

"I'd like to make an apron for one of the little girls," said Gracie.

"Well, I suppose we can. There are two girls and a boy besides the baby. Just think what a lot of trouble it must be to keep them all clothed and fed!"

"And poor 'Liza will have to do it all by herself while Ajax is in jail."

"I don't believe he was much help anyhow," said Lulu with a scornful little toss of her head. "She says he didn't work half the time and was always getting drunk and beating her and the children. I should think she'd want him kept in jail as long as he lives."

"But maybe he'll grow good and be kind and helpful to her when he gets out."

"Papa will do all he can to make him good," said Lulu. "He's gone now to the jail to talk to him. Just think of his taking so much trouble for such an ungrateful wretch."

"It's very good of him," responded Gracie. "And it's being like the dear Lord Jesus to take trouble to do good to ungrateful wretches."

"Yes, so it is, and nobody can be acquainted with papa without seeing that he tries always to be like Jesus."

The captain's motive for visiting the jail that day was certainly most kind and Christian—out of a desire to reason with the two prisoners on the sin and folly of their evil course and persuade them to repentance and reformation.

He did not approach them in a self-righteous spirit, for the thought in his heart was, "It is only the grace of God that maketh us to differ, and with the same heredity and like surroundings and influences I might have been even a greater criminal than they." But he found them sullen and defiant and by no means grateful for his kindly interest in their welfare.

Still he continued his efforts, visiting frequently while they lay in the county jail awaiting trial.

Lulu looked forward to the trial with a little bit of apprehension, dreading to be placed on the witness stand before the judges, jurymen, lawyers, and the crowd of spectators likely to be present on the occasion.

"It'll be a great, great deal worse than that time in the magistrate's office," she said to herself again and again. But by her father's advice, she tried to put away the thought of it and give her mind to other things.

She was interested in her studies, amusements, in the books and periodicals furnished for the profit and entertainment of herself and brother and sister, and in the young people's societies just started for the connection.

These prospered and grew by the addition of new members from among the young folks who, though of the neighborhood, were yet outside of the connection.

Under Grandma Elsie's both wise and kindly instruction several of the older members soon became quite expert in preparing work for themselves and the others and in gathering up information on the subject of missions and in regard to the needy of their own vicinity.

Thus their meetings were made interesting, were well attended and looked forward to with pleasure, and accomplished quite an amount of good through their means.

The Woodburn children were never willing to miss a meeting and took pride and pleasure in doing their full share of the sewing undertaken by the Dorcas society.

That was a more congenial task to Gracie than to Lulu, but the latter—partly from pride, partly from a real desire to be useful—insisted each time on carrying home at least as much work as Gracie did.

And for some weeks she was very faithful with her self-imposed task. After that her interest in that particular work began to flag, and she delayed doing it. She gave her time and thoughts to other matters, till at last Gracie reminded her that there was but a day left in which to do it, if the garments were to be ready for handing in at the next meeting of the society.

"Oh, dear!" cried Lulu. "I forgot the time was so short, and how I'm ever to finish it so soon, I don't see! I'll have to take all my play time for it."

"I wish I could help you," Gracie said with a very sympathizing look. "But you know papa said I mustn't do any more than my own."

"Of course not," returned Lulu emphatically. "Your own is too much for such a feeble little thing as you. Don't worry about me; I'll manage it somehow."

"But how can you? You have that composition to write and two lessons to learn to recite to papa in the morning. I should think they would take all your afternoon except what has been given to exercise, and it's dinner time now."

"I'll study hard and try to get the lessons and composition all done before dark, and then I'll sew as fast as I can all the evening while papa is reading or talking to Mamma Vi and us."

"I'm afraid it is more than you can do," returned Gracie with a doubtful shake of her head. "Perhaps somebody may come in to interrupt us, too."

"If they do I'll just go on with the sewing, not stopping even if there are games to be played and I'm asked to take part."

"It's nice of you to be so determined," commented Gracie, giving her sister an affectionate look.

"It's about time I was determined to do that sewing," said Lulu, laughing a little. "For I've put it off over and over again because I wanted to indulge myself in playing a game or reading a story."

The ringing of the dinner bell put a stop to their talk for a time.

At the table the captain said to his wife that business called him to the city. He must start directly when the meal was over and would not be able to get home till late, long after the usual bedtime. But he did not want anyone to sit up for him, as he could let himself in with his latchkey.

"Oh, papa," cried Lulu. "I'd like to sit up for you, if I may?"

"No, my child," he said with his pleasant smile. "I quite appreciate the kind feeling that prompts the offer, but I want you to go to your bed at the usual hour."

"Papa," observed Max insinuatingly and with an arch look, "it wouldn't hurt a boy to sit up and wait for his father."

"I'm not so sure of that," laughed the captain. "Boys need sleep as well as girls and should not be deprived of their regular allowance when there is no necessity."

"How about wives?" asked Violet with a twinkle of fun in her eye.

"Wives are, of course, not under orders," he returned gallantly, "but are free to do as they please. But I should be loath to have mine miss her beauty sleep."

"Then I suppose she should try to take it for your sake," laughed Violet.

"Papa, I wish you didn't ever, ever have to go away!" sighed Gracie. "We shall miss so much the fun with the babies and the nice talk with you while they are being put to bed and then the reading afterward."

"I have not said anything about taking the babies with me, and I really have no thought of doing so, as they would not be likely to prove of assistance in transacting my business," returned her father rather gravely.

At that, everybody laughed, and Violet said to Gracie, "So you see, dearie, you need not despair of some fun with the babies."

"Maybe not, mamma, but it won't be just the same as when papa is with us, and while you are away putting the babies to bed, we'll miss papa ever so much."

"I hope so," he said, smiling on her. "It is pleasant to feel that one's absence is regretted. But, my dear little daughter, we can't expect to have all our enjoyments every day."

"No, sir," said Lulu. "And we'll miss you when Mamma Vi comes back and you are not there to read to us."

"Of course we will," said Violet. "But though your papa is unquestionably the finest reader among us, the rest of us can read intelligibly, and some of us can read aloud to the others—perhaps we may take turns."

"A very good plan," said the captain. "But, my dear, I cannot endorse that statement of yours in regard to our relative ability as readers. I consider my wife as fine a reader as I ever listened to."

"Mamma Vi does read beautifully," remarked Max with an affectionate, admiring glance at her.

"I think so, too," assented Lulu. Then she added, "And if she will read to us it will be a great favor, and I am sure will make the time pass quickly and very pleasantly."

"No doubt," said the captain. "I am glad you are ready to appreciate such an effort on your mamma's part. But she may have other plans for the evening."

Violet had intended to spend it in writing to her absent brothers but instantly decided to sacrifice her own wishes to those of the children.

"I am sure I shall enjoy reading to so appreciative an audience," she said laughingly. "I feel myself highly honored in filling my husband's place."

"Max and Lulu," said the captain, "don't forget the tasks set for this afternoon. You can easily accomplish them before tea and have an hour or more for exercise beside."

Both replied with a promise not to forget or neglect his requirements, and immediately upon bidding her father good-bye and seeing him out of sight, Lulu went to her room and applied herself to the study of her lessons first, then to the writing of her composition.

She did her work hurriedly, however, with the thought of the sewing for which she now had so little time ever present with her. Consequently, the lessons took small hold upon her memory, and the remaining task was very indifferently performed.

She was in the act of wiping her pen when Max called to her and Gracie that the ponies were at the door and the three of them and Mamma Vi were to have a ride together.

"Oh, how very nice!" cried both little girls and hastened to don riding hats and habits.

They had grown exceedingly fond of their young stepmother, and as she did not very often find it convenient to share their rides, to have her do so was considered quite a treat.

On their return Lulu, hardly waiting to remove her outdoor garments and make herself presentable for the evening, went at the sewing with all the activity and determination of her energetic nature.

"It's got to be done if I have to work like a steam engine!" she exclaimed to Gracie, thrusting in and drawing out her needle with a rapidity that surprised her little sister.

"I never saw you sew so fast, Lu," she said. "I couldn't do it. I'd have to take more time to be sure my stitches were nice and even."

"Oh, it's for poor folks, and so it's strong. It won't make much difference about the looks," returned Lulu, working away at the same headlong pace.

"Grandma Elsie is particular about the stitches," said Gracie. "Don't you remember she told us she was, for our own sakes more than the poor folk, because it would be a sad thing for us to fall into slovenly habits of working?"

"Yes, I do remember now you speak of it, and I'll try to make the work neat as well as do it fast."

Lulu worked on, not allowing herself a moment of rest or relaxation till the tea bell rang.

Violet invited them all to spend the evening in her boudoir.

Lulu carried her sewing there directly after leaving the table, and Violet more than once spoke admiringly of the diligence and energy she displayed in working steadily on till it was time for them to separate for the night.

"It isn't done yet. Dear me, how many stitches it does take to make a garment!" sighed Lulu to Gracie when they had retired to the room of the latter.

"So it does," said Gracie. "But papa says having to take so many of them, one right after another, is a good lesson in patience and perseverance."

"Kind of lessons I'm not fond of," laughed Lulu.

"And you've worked so hard all evening! You must be very tired."

"Yes, I'm tired, but I'd sit up and work an hour or two longer if it wouldn't be disobedience to papa.

"Well, I'll see how much I can do before breakfast tomorrow morning. Perhaps I can finish. I do hope I can."

She carried out her resolution, and when their father came in for the customary bit of chat with his little daughters before breakfast, he found her sewing diligently.

He commended her industry, particularly when Gracie had told how much of it had been shown the previous evening, but he added that he hoped the tasks he had set her had been first properly attended to.

"Yes, sir, I learned my lessons and wrote my composition yesterday, before I began sewing," she replied.

"That is well," he said. "I am glad to see you willing to use some of your leisure time in working for the poor, but your education—which is to fit you for your greater usefulness in the future—must not be neglected for that or anything else."

Lulu blushed with a sudden conviction that her tasks had not been so faithfully attended to as they should have been. But it was now too late to remedy the failure, as the school hour would come very soon after breakfast and family worship.

She wished she had learned her lessons more thoroughly and spent more time and pains upon her composition, but she hoped she might be able to acquit herself better on being called to recite than she feared.

However, it proved a vain hope. She hesitated and gave incorrect answers several times in the first recitation, and when it came to the second, she showed herself entirely unacquainted with any part of the lesson.

Her father looked very grave but only said, as he handed back her book, "These are the poorest recitations I have ever heard from you."

Then taking up her composition, which he had found lying on his desk and had already examined, "And this, I am sorry to have to say, is a piece of work that does no credit to my daughter. The writing is slovenly, the sentences are badly constructed, and the spelling is very faulty. It must be re-written this afternoon, and both lessons learned so that you can recite them creditably to me before I can allow you any recreation."

"I don't care," she said with a pout and a frown. "I just have too much to do, and that's all there is about it."

"My child, are you speaking quite as respectfully as you ought in addressing your father?" he asked in grave, reproving accents.

She hung her head in sullen silence.

He waited a moment then said with sternness, "When I ask you a question, Lucilla, I expect an answer, and it must be given."

"No sir, it wasn't respectful," she replied, at once, penitent. "Please forgive me, papa. I hope I'll never speak so again."

He drew her to him and kissed her tenderly. "I do, dear child. But now I must know what you mean by saying that you have too much to do."

"It's that sewing for the Dorcas society, papa, beside all my lessons and practicing, and other things that you bid me do every day."

"Then you must undertake less of it, or none at all, for as I have said before, your lessons are of much more importance. I can pay some one to work for the poor, but my little girl's stock of knowledge must be increased and her mind improved by her own efforts."

"I don't want to give it up, papa, because it would be mortifying to have it said I couldn't so as much as the other girls."

"You seem to be doing charitable work from a very poor motive," he remarked in a tone of very grave concern.

"Papa, that isn't my only motive," she replied, hanging her head and blushing. "I do want to please the Lord Jesus and to be kind and helpful to the poor."

"I am glad to hear it, but you must be willing to undertake less if you can not do so much without neglecting other and more important duties. Did you bring home an extra quantity of work from the last meeting of your society?"

"No, sir," and she blushed again as she spoke. "But I—I kept putting off doing it because there was always something else I wanted to do—a story to read, or a game to play, or a bit of carving, or something pleasanter than sewing—till Gracie reminded me there was only one day left, and then I hurried over my lessons and composition and worked hard and fast as I could at sewing."

"Ah," he said, "it is an old and very true saying that 'Procrastination is the thief of time.' The only way to accomplish much in this world is to have a time for each duty and always attend to it at that set time.

"If you want to go on with this Dorcas work, you must set apart some particular time for it when it will not interfere with other duties and resolve not to allow yourself to use that time for anything else."

"Unless my father orders me?" she said half inquiringly, half in assertion, and with an arch look and smile.

"Yes, there may be exceptions to the rule," he replied, returning the smile.

"Now we have talked long enough on this subject and must begin to put in practice the rule I have just laid down."

"Yes, sir. I have my ciphering to do now. But, papa, must I learn the lessons over and rewrite the composition this afternoon? If you say I must, I'll have to miss the meeting of our society. I'd be very sorry for that and ashamed to have to tell why I wasn't there. Please, papa, won't you let me go and do my work over after I get back? There'll be an hour or more before tea and then all evening."

He did not answer immediately, and she added with a wistful, pleading look, "I know I don't deserve to be let go, but you've often been a great deal better to me than I deserved."

"As I well may be, considering how far beyond my deserts are my blessings," he said with a tender smile and another kiss. "Yes, daughter, you may attend the meeting, and I shall hope to hear some excellent recitations from you before you go to your bed tonight."

"Oh, thank you, dear papa! I'll try my very hardest," she exclaimed joyously, giving him a vigorous hug.

The society met at Ion that day. The captain and Violet drove over with the children, and leaving them there while they went on some miles farther, called for them again on their return at the close of the hour appropriated to its exercise.

Grandma Elsie's face hardly expressed approval as she examined Lulu's work, but she let it pass, only saying in a low aside to the little girl, "It is not quite so well done as the last garment you brought in, child, but I will overlook the partial failure, hoping the next bit of work will be an improvement upon both."

Lulu blushed and was silent. Once she would have made an angry retort, but she was slowly learning patience and humility.

On arriving at home, she set immediately to work at her tasks, nor left off till the tea bell rang. The time had been too short for her to make much progress. It was quite a trial to have to spend the whole evening in her own room while the others were enjoying the usual pleasant hours of relaxation together—the sport with the babies, the familiar chat, and interesting reading—but that, too, she bore with patience.

It was not till the call to evening worship that she joined the family. When the service was over, she drew near her father.

"Papa, I have rewritten that composition and hope you will find it a great deal better. I have studied my lessons, too, till I think I can recite them creditably."

"Ah, that is well, dear," he said, laying a hand tenderly on her head and smiling affectionately down into the eyes upraised to his. "I will go with you presently to hear the lessons and examine your little essay."

When he had done so, he said, "I am very glad indeed, daughter, to be able to bestow hearty praise on you this time. You have greatly improved your composition, and your recitations were quite perfect."

He drew her to his knee as he spoke, and she blushed with pleasure at his words.

"I missed my eldest daughter from the family circle this evening," he went on, smoothing her hair caressingly. "Indeed, I think we all missed her. I hope we will not be deprived of her company in the same way again."

"I hope not, papa. I do mean to be more faithful in preparing my lessons. I'm sure I ought when I have such a kind, kind teacher," she added, looking lovingly into his eyes. "Dear papa," putting her arm round his neck and laying her cheek to his, "I do love you so, so much!"

"My darling," he responded, "your love is very precious to me, and I don't think it can be greater than mine for you. My daughter's worth to her fond father could not be computed in dollars and cents," he added with a happy laugh.

"I hope Grandma Elsie found your sewing well done, Lulu?"

"Not so very, papa," she replied, her tone expressing some mortification. "She said it was not so nicely done as the last."

"That is a pity. It will hardly do to keep on so—going backward instead of forward with regard to improvement in that line of work."

"No, papa, I don't mean to. I didn't bring home quite so much this time, though some of the girls did look as if they thought I was growing lazy. It was dreadfully mortifying to have them think so. I'm going to try Eva's plan. She says she divides her work into as many portions as there are days to do it in, and she won't let herself miss doing at least one portion each day. She says she gets it done quite easily in that way and is often finished before the day when it is to be handed in."

"But it can't be that she puts it off for story reading, games, and what not?"

"No, sir, and I don't mean to any more. I'll put that sewing first after what you say are more important duties and not let myself have any play till it's done. I think I can 'most always do it before breakfast, now that you don't require me to sweep or dust my own room. I'm very much obliged to you, papa, for saying I needn't do those things any more while I have so many lessons."

"I want my daughters to understand all kinds of housework so that they may be competent to direct servants, if they have them, or be independent of them if they have not," he said. "But now that you have learned how to sweep and dust, I do not think it necessary for you to make use of that knowledge while your time can be better employed and I am able to pay a servant for doing the work."

CHAPTER
NINETEENTH

ONE MORNING AT breakfast, Max asked, "Papa, have you told Lu, yet?"

"No," replied the captain. "I wished her to eat her meal first in peace and comfort. Therefore, I am sorry you spoke, as I see you have now roused her curiosity."

"Yes, papa. Mayn't I know what you are talking about?" asked Lulu, giving him a disturbed, rather apprehensive look. "Oh, does the court meet today?"

"It's been meeting for several days," returned Max. "The trial of our burglars comes up today."

"And we'll have to attend as witnesses?"

"Yes, but you needn't be alarmed. You ought to be quite used to it since your experience in the magistrate's office," answered Max sportively.

"I don't think I'd ever get used to it, and I just wish there was some way to keep out of it!" sighed Lulu.

"But as there isn't, my little girl will make up her mind to go through with it bravely," the captain said, giving her an encouraging smile.

"I'll try, papa," she answered but with a sigh that sounded rather hopeless.

Violet anad Gracie both expressed their deepest sympathy, but they were sure Lulu would do herself credit, as she had on the former occasion.

Lulu brightened a little and went on with her meal. "How soon do we have to go, papa?" she asked.

"In about half an hour after breakfast," he answered. "That will take us to the town for the opening of today's session of the court. We may not be called on for our testimony for hours, but we must be on hand in case we are wanted."

Lulu wasted no more breath in vain wishes or objections, but her usual flow of spirits had deserted her. As they drove toward the town, her father noticed that she was very quiet and that her face wore a look of patient resignation and fortitude as if she had made up her mind to go courageously through a difficult and trying ordeal.

"Don't be anxious and troubled, dear child," he said, taking her hand and pressing it affectionately in his. "You are not going alone into that crowded court room."

"No, papa, and I'm so glad you will be with me."

"And not only I, but a nearer, dearer, and more powerful Friend. Jesus says, 'Lo, I am with you always, even unto the end of the world.' He says it to every one of His disciples, and that always must include this time that you are dreading.

"He will be close beside you, and you can ask Him at any instant for the help you need to know exactly what to say and do — the help to be calm and collected and to answer both clearly and perfectly truthfully every question put to you."

"Papa, it's so nice to think of that!" she exclaimed, looking up brightly and with glad tears shining in her eyes. "Thank you so very much for reminding me of it. Now I shall not be at all afraid, even if the lawyers do ask me hard, puzzling questions, as I've read in the papers that they do to witnesses sometimes."

"No, you need not be afraid. I am not afraid for you, for I am sure you will be helped to say just what you ought. And if—as I believe will happen— you are enabled to acquit yourself well, remember, when people commend you for it, that having done so by help from on high, the honor is not fairly due to you. And you have no reason to be conceited and vain in consequence."

"I hope I'll be kept from being that, papa," she returned. "I don't think that for anybody with as good a memory as mine, having told a straight-forward, truthful story is anything to be puffed up about."

"No, certainly not."

The wealth and standing in the community of Captain Raymond and his wife's relatives caused a widespread interest in the case about to be tried— especially in connection with the fact that he and two of his children were to be placed on the witness stand to testify to the identity of the burglars and their attempt to rob his house.

The Court House was crowded, and there were many people among the spectators, including members of the families residing at the Oaks, the Laurels, the Pines, Ion, Fairview, and Roselands.

Dr. Conly, Mr. and Mrs. Edward Travilla, and Mr. Leland were there when the Woodburn party arrived. Presently Grandpa Dinsmore, Grandma Rose, and Cousin Ronald, who was still staying at Ion, followed.

These all sat near together, and Lulu felt it a comfort to find herself in the midst of such a company of friends.

Greetings were exchanged, and some kind and encouraging words were spoken to her and Max, then their father and the other gentlemen fell into conversation.

The children had never been in a courtroom before, and they were interested in looking about and observing what was going on. They were early—in season to see the judges come in and take their seats on the bench and the opening of the court.

Some lesser matters occupied its attention for a time, then there was a little stir of excitement in the crowd as the sheriff and his deputy entered with Ajax and his fellow burglar, but it quieted down in a moment as the prisoners took their places at the bar. The voice of the presiding judge sounded distinctly through the room: "Commonwealth against Perry Davis and Ajax Stone. Burglary. Are you ready for trial?"

"We are, your honor," replied the district attorney.

"Very well," said the judge, "arraign the prisoners."

Then the two prisoners were told to stand up while the district attorney read the indictment, which charged them with "burglariously breaking and entering into the house of Captain Raymond of Woodburn on the second day of January last passed," and while there attempting to break into and rob his safe and to carry off articles of value from other parts of the dwelling.

The courtroom was very quiet during the reading of the indictment, so that Max and Lulu who were listening intently, heard every word.

Lulu looked her astonishment when the prisoners pleaded, "Not guilty."

"Why they are! And they know they are!" she whispered to Max.

"Of course," he returned in the same low key. "But do you suppose men who break into houses to steal will hesitate to lie?"

"Oh, no, to be sure not! How silly I am!"

The next thing was the selecting of the jurors—a rather tedious business taking up all the rest of the time till the court adjourned for the noon recess.

That was a rest for Max and Lulu. Their father took them to a hotel for lunch, and they chattered a while in its parlor after satisfying their appetites then returned to the courtroom in season for the opening of the afternoon session.

The district attorney made the opening address, giving an outline of the evidence he expected to bring forward to prove the prisoners' guilt. Then Lulu was called to the witness stand.

She rose at once and turned to her father, looking a trifle pale, but she seemed quite calm and collected.

He took her hand and led her to the little railed platform. She stepped up on it, and he stood near to encourage her by his presence.

"You are very young, child," the judge said in a kindly tone. "What know you of the nature of an oath?"

"I know, sir, that it is a very solemn promise in the presence of the great God, to tell the truth, the whole truth, and nothing but the truth."

"What will happen if you fail to do so, my dear?"

"God will know it and be angry, for He hates lying and has said, 'All liars shall have their part in the lake that burneth with fire and brimstone!'"

Lulu's answers were given in a low, but very distinct tone, and in the almost breathless silence were quite audible in every part of the large room.

"Administer the oath to her," said the judge, addressing the clerk of the court. "She is more competent to take it than many an older person."

When she had done so, "What is your name?" asked the district attorney.

"Lucilla Raymond."

"And you are the daughter of Captain Levis Raymond, late of the United States Navy?"

"Yes, sir, his eldest daughter."

"How old are you?"

"I was twelve on my last birthday, last summer."

"Look at the prisoners. Have you ever seen them before, Lucilla?"

"Yes, sir."

"When and where?"

"The colored man has lived in our family, and I saw him every day for months."

"And the white man?"

"I have seen him three times before today—first on the second day of last January, when my brother and I were riding home through the bit of wood on my father's estate. That man was leaning against a tree, and my pony nearly stepped on him before I knew he was there. He seized her bridle and said, fiercely, 'Look out there and don't ride a fellow down!'"

"And what did you answer?"

"Let go of my bridle this instant and get out of the path!"

"Plucky!" laughed someone in the audience.

"What happened next?" asked the lawyer. And Lulu went on to tell the whole story of their adventure in the wood.

"That, you have told us, was your first sight of the prisoner calling himself Perry Davis. When did you see him next? And where?"

"That night in what we call the strong room where papa's safe is."

She was bidden to tell the whole of that story also and did so in the same clear, straightforward manner in which she told it in the magistrate's office. She told it simply, artlessly—as not aware of the bravery and unselfishness of her conduct in attempting the capture of the burglars at the risk of being attacked and murdered by them—and in the same calm, even, distinct tones in which she had spoken at first.

A murmur of great admiration ran through the courtroom as she concluded her narrative with, "Papa was asleep, and I couldn't speak just at first for want of breath. But when I put my arm round his neck and laid my face on the pillow beside his, he woke, and I told him about the burglars and what I had done."

The prisoners had listened with close attention and evident interest.

"So 'twas her—that chit of a gal that fastened us in—caught us in a trap, as one may say," muttered Davis, scowling at her and grinding his teeth in rage. "Pity I didn't hold on to that ere bridle and kerry her off afore we ventur'd in thar."

A warning look from his counsel silenced him, and the latter addressed himself to Lulu.

"You said you had seen Davis three times before today. Where and when did you see him the third time?"

"In the magistrate's office, the next morning after he and Ajax had been in our house."

"Did you then recognize them as the same men you had seen in the strong room of your home the night before at work at the lock of the safe?"

"Yes, sir, and Davis as the man who had seized my pony's bridle in the wood."

"But you had not seen Ajax Stone's face. How then could you recognize him?"

"No, I had not seen his face, but I had the back of his head and how he was dressed. I knew I had fastened him in there, and that he didn't get out till the sheriff took him out. And I heard his voice and knew it was Ajax's voice."

The cross questioning went on. This was what Lulu had dreaded, but it did not seem to embarrass or disturb her, nor could she be made to contradict herself at all.

Her father's eyes shone. He looked a proud and happy man as he led her back to her seat, holding her hand in a tender, loving clasp.

She was surprised and pleased to find Grandma Elsie and Violet sitting with the other relatives and friends. They had come in while she was on the witness stand.

"Dear child," Violet said, making room for her by her side, "you went through your ordeal very gracefully, and I am very glad for your sake that it is over."

"Yes, my dear, we are all proud of you," added Grandma Elsie, smiling kindly upon the little girl.

But there was not time for anything more.

"Max Raymond," someone called.

"Here, sir," replied the lad, rising.

"Take the witness stand."

"Go, my son, and let us see how well you can acquit yourself," the captain said in an encouraging tone, and Max obeyed.

He also conducted himself quite to his father's satisfaction, behaving in a very manly way and giving his testimony in the same clear, distinct tomes and straightforward manner that had been admired in his sister. But having much less to tell, he was not kept nearly so long upon the stand.

There were other witnesses for the prosecution, one of whom was Captain Raymond himself.

He testified that the burglars had evidently entered the house through a window, by prying open a shutter, removing a pane of glass, then reaching in, and turning the catch over the lower sash.

When the evidence on that side had all been heard, the counsel for the accused opened the case for the defense.

He was an able and eloquent lawyer, but his clients had already established an unenviable reputation for themselves, and the weight of the evidence against them was too strong for rebuttal. Their conviction was a foregone conclusion in his mind, and that of almost everyone present, even before he began his speech.

He had but few witnesses to bring forward, and their testimony was unimportant and availed nothing as disproof of that given by those for the prosecution.

After the lawyers on both sides had addressed the jury, and the judge had delivered his charge to them, they retired to consider their verdict.

In only a few moments they returned and resumed their seats in the jury box. They found both the accused guilty of burglary, and the trial was over.

"Is it quite finished, papa?" Lulu asked as they were driving toward home again.

"What, my child? The trial? Yes, there will be no more of it."

"I'm so glad!" she exclaimed with a sigh of relief. "You said they would have to go to the penitentiary if they were found guilty, and the jury said they were. How long will they have to stay there?"

"I don't know. They have not been sentenced yet, but it will be for some years."

"I'm sorry for them. I wish they hadn't been so wicked, papa."

"So do I."

"And that I hadn't had to testify against them. I can't help feeling as though it was unkind, and that their friends have a right to hate me for it."

"No, not at all. It was a duty you owed the community—because to allow criminals to go unpunished would make honest people unsafe—and indeed, to the men themselves, as being brought to justice may prove the means of their reformation. So set your mind at rest about it, my darling. Try to forget the whole unpleasant affair and be happy in the enjoyment of your many blessings."

"There is one thing that helps to make my conscience perfectly easy on the score of having testified against them," remarked Max. "And that is I couldn't help myself but had to obey the law."

"True enough," rejoined his father. "And Lulu was no more a free agent than yourself."

"No, sir. But she did more to catch the rogues than anybody else," Max went on, giving her a merry, laughing glance. "Don't you wish, sis, that you had let them go on and help themselves to all they wanted and then leave without being molested?"

"No, I don't," she answered with spirit. "I wouldn't want papa to lose his money or Mamma Vi her jewels. Besides they might have gone upstairs and hurt some of us."

"We are all much obliged to you, Lulu, dear," Violet remarked, looking affectionately at the little girl. "How brave and unselfish you were! That burglary following so immediately upon the festivities of our delightful Christmas holidays seemed a most trying and unfortunate afterclap, but we will hope for better things next time."

The End